K

D

Donated by

FUNDS PROVIDED

BY

THE

DODGEVILLE TOWNSHIP

Sheriff of Cow County

**Center Point
Large Print**

**This Large Print Book carries the
Seal of Approval of N.A.V.H.**

Sheriff of Cow County

Lauran Paine

Center Point Publishing
Thorndike, Maine

This Center Point Large Print edition
is published in the year 2002 by arrangement with
Golden West Literary Agency.

Copyright © 1962 by Lauran Paine in the British Commonwealth.
Copyright © 2002 by Mona Paine.

All rights reserved.

The text of this Large Print edition is unabridged. In other
aspects, this book may vary from the original edition. Printed in
Thailand. Set in 16-point Times New Roman type by
Bill Coskrey and Gary Socquet.

ISBN 1-58547-207-7

Library of Congress Cataloging-in-Publication Data.

Paine, Lauran.
    Sheriff of Cow County / Lauran Paine.--Center Point large print ed.
        p. cm.
    Originally published under John Kilgore. 1962.
    ISBN 1-58547-207-7 (lib. bdg. : alk. paper)
        1. Sheriffs--Fiction. 2. Large type books. I. Title.

PS3566.A34 S49 2002
813'.54--dc21

                                                        2002020038

CHAPTER ONE

THE NIGHT was crisp and cool, and overhead fresh-scrubbed stars hung in a rain-washed sky, burning with sharp intensity. Out a ways, east of Vacaville, Blue River pushed its crested swell, rain-swollen and freshet-fed, between the cut-banks, a twisted, broad band of silver beneath the leaning moon, and yonder where the mountains stood stark and twisted, layer after layer of them, a hard darkness lay.

There was a stillness to the vault of heaven, and lower, where the big land ran out soft in the moonlight, it was the same, and even in Vacaville where lamp-light leavened darkness from two score stores, there was a depth of unnatural quiet. Some noticed, some did not; some, like Antonia Parker, moving toward Doctor McMahon's office on Front Street, passed through stillness without being aware of it.

She came onto the plankwalk from the dust of Grant Street, easterly, with the tap of her heels drumming out swift echoes, and the tall man leaning against the front of McMahon's office, tired shoulders tipped back against the boards, straightened up. He touched his hat before her face was visible in the gloom under the overhang, and spoke in a quiet-gentle way.

" 'Evening, Toni . . ." He was a tall, weathered man, with a face made hard by life, and dead-level grey eyes. On his shirtfront a nickel circlet showed with a star within it.

"Sheriff . . . I came as soon as I heard."

"You're in time. I been standing out here listening. Pat's

doing all he can."

They heard someone inside cry out a word, and Antonia Parker went past, entered the office and closed the door silently. The sheriff let out a long, pent up breath, and blurred into the shadows, striding north toward *Householder's Saloon.*

The man on the leather couch rolled his head at the swish of skirts and the quick tap of heels. Doctor Pat McMahon, the sheriff's brother, got out of his chair beside the couch and moved back by the desk, turning completely around as he did so, because he did not wish to see this.

Antonia knelt by the couch, and the man there, young Reed Benton, looked up at her out of drowsy, puzzled blue eyes, and from the loosening thickness of his throat, he said, "Toni . . ."

She took a limp hand and held it between her palms, pressingly, and although she did not speak it was plain on her face what filled her mind. She raised her head, turned it looking at Doctor McMahon's back. Then Reed Benton murmured her name again, and spoke.

"I'm glad you're here."

"How did it happen?"

He appeared not to hear. His head rolled on the leather, he moistened dry lips, greying now, and faintly framed words on them. "It's good you're here, Toni. My beautiful Toni." He breathed shallowly, painfully, and she heard the fading tone. "Don't—forget me."

She saw him loosen; heard him sigh; watched the drowsy smile settle indelibly. Then there was no movement. She pressed the cooling hand harder, harder, and in he⌷⌷⌷⌷ eyes, dark now and large with fear, there was a loc⌷⌷⌷⌷

a deep faith broken.

Doctor McMahon had turned. He was still and slumped in his rumpled sack-suit, and he was holding his right wrist with the locked fingers of his left hand.

Stillness piled up and pressed downwards in the room. Even the tinkle of music from the north end of town didn't intrude. McMahon loosened the grip on his arm, moved ahead and felt Reed Benton's pulse. Antonia Parker did not see him, even when he lay the limp arm back down. She didn't hear him tip-toe across the room and leave by the front entrance. His diminishing footfalls grew fainter, and when he stopped outside *Carleton's Casino*, looking somberly over the doors, there was a hard look of resignation across his face.

Doctor Pat McMahon didn't enter *Carleton's*. Through the smoke of the place he saw a man at the bar, a thickly made man drinking with other cowboys. He moved back and went farther along the plankwalk, as far as *Householder's Saloon*. There, he pushed inside, the rush of heat and smells and talk rolling off him as he went to the bar and hung there, elbows planted, legs sprung at the knees, eyes unseeing in the back-bar mirror.

"Sour mash, Doc?"

A slight nod.

As the barman moved away a looming hulk, as tall as Pat McMahon, edged in beside him. The face was bony and lined, but the nose and mouth and eyes were the same.

"Is he dead?"

The doctor nodded, recognising his brother's voice. "Y.. he's dead."

W... the sour mash came the sheriff regarded it a

7

moment, then jutted his chin downward and bobbed his head at the barman. "The same, Will."

"Sure, Sheriff."

Pat picked up his glass, felt its oiliness, and threw back his head. Then he put the glass down and twisted from the waist. "And the law calls that a fair fight," he said with flinty softness.

Sheriff McMahon shrugged, eyes fixed on the barman who was bringing his drink. "They were both armed, Pat, and Reed's gun was half out when Porter Buel fired."

"Reed never stood a chance and the whole damned town knows it."

The sheriff drank, shuddered, and turned the empty glass in a pool of dampness on the bartop. He said nothing.

"And of course the Skull Valley men stand by Buel."

"Pat," the Sheriff said patiently, "Buel had seven witnesses. Three of them were townsmen. Four were Skull Valley riders. He had a fair-and-square hearing."

"Self-defence," Doctor McMahon said with bitterness. "Dammit, Mike; you grew up with Reed. Even in school he was awkward. And when we used to go hunting, four or five of us, he couldn't hit the side of a barn with a gun. He was a horseman, Mike, not a gunfighter. Why; it'd be the same if I went up against Porter Buel."

"Listen, Pat; don't do anything foolish."

"I'm not going to. I just don't see how——"

"I know, I know," the sheriff interrupted to say. "Everybody in town feels the same way. But Pat; don't you get het up, too. Buel killed him fair."

"Is that all you can say?" the doctor demanded.

His brother raised the glass in his hand and put it down,

hard. "No, it's not all I can say. It isn't all I can think, either—but it's all I can *do* about it. I'm just the sheriff, Pat; I'm not the judge." Sheriff Mike McMahon's wide mouth drew out thin. "And if I'd been the judge I'd have found Buel clear of blame just like he did." Mike's level eyes raised. "I wish you—and the rest like you—would get one thing through your heads. I know how you feel, and I feel the same way—dammit; I've known Reed all my life too—but he went for his gun. *He went for his gun*—get that into your thick skull."

"Yeh; he went for his gun. Buel forced him to do it, and now he's dead down there at my place with Antonia Parker kneeling beside the couch." The doctor flagged for a refill and pushed his glass forward. "When I was in medical school the Dean wanted me to stay in Chicago and practice. He said it was a waste of talent for me to come back out here. I think he was right."

"The same thing could've happened in Chicago."

"No. They've got police there. People don't go around wearing guns and spoiling for a chance to use them."

"All *right!* Why the hell didn't you stay?" The sheriff started to turn away. Anger put colour into his sun-darkened cheeks. Doctor McMahon caught his arm and held on.

"Mike; take my word for it. This isn't settled."

The grey eyes drew up level and steady. "Now you listen to me, Pat. I've had about enough interference over this thing. I won't stand for much more, not even from you. If you're thinking about keeping things stirred up—forget it. I'll lock you up just like anyone else. Now you remember that."

The doctor wasn't aware of the stillness until his brother was walking toward the door; then he saw the raised faces, hushed and expectant. He turned back toward the bar and nodded for another drink.

Outside, Sheriff Mike stood in the coolness breathing deeply. A troubled anger lay in his eyes and down across his face. Riders jogged past and invisible black dust scuffed to life behind them. The lights at the bakery were unusually bright; people were working there, kneading up batches of bread for the next day's trade. Southward, he saw a bareheaded woman walking with her head down. She passed the liverybarn, the bakery, the smoking lights of the Mexican beanery, and at the alley which cut back behind the liverybarn, she turned into the shadows, sinking away from sight. He thought he knew who it was, but wondered; what would Antonia Parker be going into a dark alley for—and this night of all nights.

Down at *Carleton's Casino* a crashing ring of fierce profanity arose over the diminishing murmur of voices. Sheriff Mike half turned. At that moment a man rocketed out into the moonlighted roadway, sprawling. His voice, thin and high as a child's voice, made a forlorn echo on the night air. Sheriff Mike started forward, stepping solidly on the plankwalk. He had his head up, illuminated by moonlight. His expression was carved granite-like; hard and a little cruel.

When the *Casino's* spindled-door shivered outwards Sheriff Mike caught the first man out with one iron hand, drew him sideways off balance, pulling him so close the cowboy could not draw his gun. The scent of whiskey was strong and stifling; the rider's leathery face was working in a blending of anger and surprise. Sheriff Mike threw him back forcibly.

"*You!* Damn you, Buel; you've caused enough trouble for one day. Get your horse and your friends and get out of town—now!"

Porter Buel was a rock-like man, thickly massive and squat. He had a great-thrusting jaw which dominated an otherwise nondescript face, and his eyes, bloodshot now and unduly wet, focused on Sheriff McMahon with slow attentiveness. Behind him, men stood still, as startled by McMahon's appearance and obvious wrath, as Buel was. When Buel did not move Sheriff Mike reached for him. The Skull Valley rider twisted away.

"Yeh; I'm going," he said, and moved ponderously through the others, bound for the hitchrail. From beside his horse he looked back and spoke. "Listen, McMahon; if you're figuring on ridin' me for that fight with Benton— don't. Just don't, that's all. You don't scare me one bit." Buel mounted, looked at the men on the plankwalk, jerked his head at them and spun his horse.

When the other Skull Valley men were riding out, south- ward, in the wake of Porter Buel, Sheriff Mike turned away. A voice reached for him from the diminishing onlookers.

"Mike?"

He turned, watching the speaker push forward. It was Hugh Grant, a once-powerful man now running to fat, who owned Vacaville's most prosperous smithy—*Grant's Forge.*

"How's Reed?"

"Dead."

Grant walked northward beside McMahon without speaking for a moment. Then he cleared his throat and spat into the dust. "Too bad. I recollect him as a kid hanging around my shop."

The sheriff said nothing. They walked as far as *Nolan's Saddle & Harness Shop*, and there Hugh Grant halted, legs spread wide. "There's some talk, Mike."

"There always is, Hugh."

"I reckon."

"If folks had wanted to jump Buel they had all afternoon to do it."

Grant's deep-set, small eyes looked up. They were drawn out narrow in speculation. "No; nobody'd jump him with those other five Skull Valleyers with him."

"Then they didn't want him very bad, Hugh."

"They want him, Mike. They'll get him, too. But when he's alone."

"Not in town," Sheriff Mike said. "Beyond town limits I don't care what folks do—providing it's not too illegal."

"Your authority's county-wide, Mike."

Mike McMahon studied the older man closely. "What're you driving at, Hugh? You know how things operate here-abouts—one sheriff, no deputies—murders, robberies, rustling. Yes—fair-fights—No."

"They're going to catch Buel alone and lynch him. I heard the talk tonight." The sheriff looked disgusted. Hugh Grant's face lengthened. "No; they mean it. They'll do it, Mike, sure as I'm a foot high."

"Who'll do it?"

Grant's gaze slipped off McMahon's face and went out into the dark roadway. "Don't recollect," he said.

"Then why tell me about it?"

"Because you can stop it. Tell Buel to stay out of Vacaville and away from the folks hereabouts—at least for a month or two."

"Why d'you care what happens to Porter Buel?"

Grant looked up again. "I don't. Not really, Mike. I just don't hold with lynch-law."

"Were you at Reed's inquest today?"

"Yes; I was there."

"And you saw how Buel got off—when everyone knows how he forced Reed into that fight?"

"I saw."

Sheriff Mike looked down and his voice was quiet. "I don't care a whoop what happens to Porter Buel, Hugh. Not a whoop." McMahon turned on his heel and walked away.

Hugh Grant watched him pause outside the saloon of Charley Householder, then pass on to fade into the night. He drew out a cigar, lit it, and blew out a great lungful of fragrant smoke. A man who had lived as long on the frontier as Hugh Grant had, developed an intuitive feeling about trouble. Grant had that feeling now; strong, too. He turned and began walking toward the intersection of Fifth Street, which ran east and west. When he was near the juncture, he saw a dark shadow sweep from beyond the alley and pause, face lifted and turning. Moonlight fell across the even, lovely features of Antonia Parker. Hugh Grant halted in surprise; remained motionless until the girl turned, heading south, then he smoked for a long, thoughtful moment, before resuming his way homeward. The feeling was stronger now; there was going to be trouble, whether Mike McMahon thought so or not.

The night caught sounds from Vacaville's two large saloons and carried them upwards. Overhead, whitely glistening stars shone, and the ragged moon moved glidingly below the immense curve of heaven. Mike McMahon, strolling through the night fragrance, came abreast of two gesticulating Mexicans. One was obviously a townsman; a merchant of some kind. The other was just as clearly a rancher. Both were of middle age, burnt Apache-black by the sun of their native Arizona, and, as Mike came up, both turned toward him, letting their voices dwindle down to silence. Finally, the leaner, darker of the two, made a gesture of appeal and spoke.

"Sheriff; you know Epifanio here. He says we must not have the fiesta this week. He says there is going to be trouble—that we should put it off until, maybe, next month." There was protest in the voice. Protest and an appeal for support.

Mike looked searchingly into the face of the second man. Dark eyes met his only briefly then skidded away. "What kind of trouble, 'Pifas?"

"Trouble, Sheriff," the second Mexican replied with an eloquent shrug. "The shooting today of the man who owned the liverybarn. There is formidable feeling—much talk," another shrug; the liquid dark eyes lifted finally, and rested on Mike's face. "It is a small thing to postpone the fiesta. It is more important that it make money."

"*Si,*" the Mexican cowman said, rolling his eyes heavenward. "Every year since my father's time—since my grandfather's time—the fiesta has been held in this week of each year—now, it must not lose money. It must be very successful. Is money so permanent then that everything else must bow to it? Only to merchants, Sheriff; only to Epifanio."

"'Pifas," Sheriff Mike said quietly, seeing the troubled look on the face before him. "I don't think there'll be trouble over the shooting of Reed Benton. At least, not serious trouble. But if there was big trouble, don't you think it would draw people to the fiesta—not scare them away?"

"Oh no, *Señor.* Such a thing is not so. People don't wish to be where bullets are flying. Not during a fiesta—no, no."

"I doubt if bullets will fly," the sheriff said dryly. "At least no more than usual."

The merchant's brow furrowed in doubt, but his tone changed subtly. "You know there is nothing to this talk against the men of Skull Valley, then, Sheriff?"

"I don't know, of course not; but I don't think it means anything. Folks usually get upset over a killing. Anyway; if they'd wanted Buel, they could've gotten him today—he hung around town all afternoon, 'Pifas."

"I see. You believe this?"

"Yes, I believe it."

Another shrug, this time directed toward the rancher. "*Si;* I withdraw my objections then."

The cowman's white teeth flashed in the moonlight. He winked a dark eye at Sheriff Mike, from a face turned blandly triumphant. "*Duerme,* Sheriff; time was when trouble came and went—," the rancher's shoulders drooped down, his hands came forward, palms upwards "—and still the moon rose, the heat came, the fiesta was held, and people did not hide in fear, nor change the pattern

15

of their lives." The smile faded; the dark eyes fixed themselves upon the merchant, and the rancher's breath whipsawed outward. "But now—you see what passes?—times do not change, but men do. *Adios, Señores; buenas noches, good night.*"

Sheriff Mike and the merchant watched the rancher walk away, go to a horse at *Householder's* hitchrail, mount up and spin away. Then Epifanio sighed audibly and wagged his head.

"If God is willing," he said in Spanish, "trouble will not pass," then he switched to English and gazed steadily at Sheriff Mike. "But there was the *Señorita* Antonia and that man . . . I think there must be something you do not know, Sheriff."

Mike saw the fatalistic expression and understood it fully. He pushed his question out sharply. "What do you mean—what man?"

"Hubbel—the one who works at the liverybarn. The tall, blond man."

"Hank Hubbel? What about him, 'Pifas?"

"It was a small thing, Sheriff, and of a certainty none of my affair. This man met the *Señorita* Antonia behind the bakery tonight. I know; I saw them from the kitchen of my cafe. They talked. They spoke together for a long time, then Hubbel rode west, out of town."

"You must've been mistaken," the sheriff said, his face darkening into a scowl. "Some other girl. Hell, 'Pifas; it's dark out."

"True; it's dark out. But I am not mistaken."

"Antonia Parker?" The sheriff scoffed. "Naw; not a chance. What would Antonia be talking with a whelp like

Hubbel for?"

The merchant swung his gaze away. He said no more, and finally, he walked away.

Sheriff Mike went back to his office, dropped down at the table, made a cigarette and smoked it. His gaze was fixed sightlessly upon the opposite adobe wall. It moved off only when Doctor Pat entered the room, weaving a little and wearing a greyish look on his face. The sheriff grunted under his breath and got up, heading for the wood-stove and the coffeepot upon it. Over his shoulder, and with spite, he said, "Too bad your Chicago Dean can't see you now. Sit down over there on the bench."

The doctor sat down dutifully and regarded his brother's back steadily. Then he made a crooked smile. "Too bad the Dean can't see Vacaville—he wouldn't believe it. He wouldn't believe it for a fact." The smile faded and the tired, damp eyes moved around the room. "Have you seen Toni?"

"No; why should I see her?"

"She isn't sane."

Sheriff Mike turned, the coffeepot poised. "What?"

"That's right. You heard me. Well—pour the coffee or put the pot down."

Mike filled a tin cup, two tin cups, crossed to his table and put one down there, then went across to his brother and held the other cup out. "What do you mean—she isn't sane?"

"Just that. Ouch! This stuff is scalding-hot."

"I thought you'd be too drunk to notice."

Doctor Pat looked across at his brother. "I'm not drunk," he said. "Not the way you mean. Sure; I've been drinking—but I'm not drunk—I'm sick to my stomach."

"Well, go outside." Mike said tartly. "What do you mean, about Toni?"

"Can't you get it through your thick skull—she's out of her mind. She's been walking—all over town—in the dark. Looking right through folks, saying nothing to anyone—crazy—insane."

"How d'you know she hasn't talked to anyone?"

"I know," the doctor said, finishing the coffee and grimacing at its bitterness. "I know because I know the symptoms. Temporary insanity caused by grief. It happens—especially to women." He put the cup aside and flagged an arm at the sheriff. "Sometimes they never come out of it—but that's usually when they're middle-aged. Toni'll come out of it . . . Then you know what? Then she'll be different. She'll have changed, Mike. Changed."

"You're not making much sense," the sheriff said. "Why don't you go home? By the way—when are you going to bury Reed?"

Doctor Pat looked hard at his brother and got awkwardly to his feet still staring. He said, "I don't understand you. I don't understand you at all. Reed was a fellow you grew up with. You've known him all your life; he was your *friend,* Mike. He was a part of your life, like I am. Is it only important that you know when he's to be buried?"

Mike McMahon's grey-level stare got sharp. His body stiffened in the chair. "Go on home, Pat. Get some rest."

"You—."

"Now that's enough. You get along home. Close your mouth—not another damned word." Mike stood up. "Now go along."

Doctor Pat went as far as the door. There he turned back, one hand fumbling at the latch. "I know what it is; you're used to dead people and I'm not. Not yet, anyway. Reed's dead—that's all."

"No, that isn't all. Can I bring him back to life? Can you? Of course not. Then, you stew in your kind of juice and I'll stew in mine."

"Yeah?" The doctor said softly. "And what kind of juice'll Porter Buel stew in?"

"You'll see. Before this is over for him it'll be worse than it is for either you or me. Now go on home—and Pat— never mind leaving the lamp burning. I won't be along for a while yet."

After his brother had departed, the sheriff scooped up his hat, tugged it on and went out into the night. It was late; there was very little noise, even from the *Casino* or *Householder's Saloon.* Nearly all the hitchrails were empty. Softly, riding muted on the night air, came guitar music from the Mexican quarter of Vacaville. Mike McMahon angled across the roadway heading south toward Grant Street. When he was passing the darkened houses, his mind was busy with fragments of things he had heard—and with something he, himself, had seen, but had not believed, until now.

The Parker place was as dark as its neighbours. Sheriff Mike went quietly up to the porch, eased down on a chair and thrust his legs far out. He was tired in mind and body and the longer he waited, the more looseness settled upon him. Then he heard it again, the quick, hard tapping of a woman's footfalls. He drew up a little, waiting.

A shadow came closer down the roadway. It bent sharply

at the gate and started toward the house. Mike arose suddenly, blocking the doorway. The girl stifled an outcry, staring whitely up into his dark and shadowed face.

"Where have you been, Toni?" Sheriff Mike asked evenly, his voice softly deep.

She made as if to brush past. McMahon remained solidly before the door, looking down at her.

"I want to know where you've been tonight."

"I . . . It doesn't matter."

"Yes, it does. Where did you send Hank Hubbel?"

Wide blue eyes flashed to his face, oddly hard and shining. "What are you talking about? Don't you know what they've done to Reed?"

"Yes, I know, Toni. Is that why you sent Hubbel out of town?"

"Get out of my way."

He reached out, touched her arm gently, and watched her recoil from the contact. The hand fell away to his side. "Listen to me, Toni; Hank Hubbel can't do anything about Reed's death. He's only—"

"Yes he can," she said swiftly, vehemently, the words rushing out all together. "He worked for Reed. He liked him. He's running the liverybarn now. He can do it."

"Do what?"

"Do what you won't do."

Sheriff Mike's gaze didn't waver. "I see," he said in the same quiet tone. "You think Hubbel can match Port Buel—well—he can't. Buel could down him with one hand. I'm surprised he'd do this—for Reed, or you."

"Are you? Not everyone in Vacaville's afraid of those Skull Valleyers. Not everyone, Sheriff."

"Listen, Toni—please listen to me." She was twisting away, but his voice held her. "Buel will kill Hubbel in a fair fight. If Hubbel's aiming to bushwack Buel—I'll find out about it. If he succeeds, he'll be guilty of murder, and you'll be an accomplice to murder. Do you understand what I'm telling you?"

"Perfectly, yes. Now—please get out of my way."

Mike moved aside. As the girl swung past he caught her arm and held it, tightly. "Toni; what's got into you? We grew up together. You know I—"

"Let me go." She pulled away, glaring up at him. "You don't know . . . You're like the rest of them—you talk about what Buel did—and it's just talk."

"Hank Hubbel can't help—"

"Hank isn't going to kill Buel. He isn't even going near him. Now—" a sob racked her; she wrenched at the door, disappeared inside, leaving Sheriff Mike McMahon looking at the closed door in a puzzled way.

He returned uptown. Vacaville was hushed and darkened. He made his customary patrol of the hitchrails to make sure no passed-out cowboy had forgotten his horse, found the rails empty, then retraced his steps to the sheriff's office, locked up for the night, and started for the home he shared with his brother.

The night was turning crisply cold and there was a faint sighing of ground-breeze rustling the dust, and fluting upwards to rattle loose shingles. Stars shone with cold brilliance; the moon was listing off-centre. A narrow cloud-banner scudded below it, distantly pale and thin. Sheriff Mike turned in past the sagging gate thinking that Reed Benton should be buried before the fiesta commenced, to eliminate an intermingling of two opposite and clashing sentiments; sadness and gaiety.

He looked up, noted that the house was dark, and a faint smile touched his lips. Doctor Pat would have a headache in the morning.

CHAPTER TWO

SHERIFF MIKE was out of town on Wednesday, the day of Reed Benton's funeral. He did not return until late Wednesday night. At the liverybarn a nighthawk told him all about it. It seemed that even the Mexicans, who rarely mixed in the affairs of the American part of Vacaville, had marched solemnly in the procession, and the funeral was, all agreed, the most impressive turn-out Vacaville had ever witnessed; bigger even than the annual Fourth of July Celebrations.

Mike saw Hank Hubbel in the barn-office, but he did not speak to him. It was enough that Hubbel had returned. As he walked wearily out into the night, he thought that prudence had probably kept Hubbel from challenging Porter Buel. He was smiling dourly over that as he strode south toward the office.

Several Mexican merchants were waiting for him. They arose when he entered, tossed his hat upon the antler-rack and nodded to them, scratching his head.

"'Evening, gentlemen. What can I do for you?"

"The fiesta, Sheriff; it begins tomorrow."

"All right. Fine. What about it?"

"Well; because we wish no trouble, we wish to make sure

22

there will be none."

Mike stood looking at the Mexicans a moment, then went to his chair behind the table and sank down. He, also, was a native of Arizona, and he knew Mexicans as well as he knew the cowmen and the Apaches. They said things in their own way, and in their own good time. He sat there looking up and waiting.

"We have a young man we wish you to deputise. He will help you during the celebration. He is a good young man—and he is of course formidable with a gun."

"I don't think I'll need him," Mike said.

"But Sheriff; he is not troublesome. He is quiet and of good manners and he is very brave. He could patrol the fiesta after dark, too. We ask that you talk to him."

Mike shrugged. "All right. Have him come by in the morning."

"He is outside now."

Mike's brows drew down. "I didn't see anyone outside."

"He is waiting."

"All right; bring him in. You fellers can go on home. I'll talk to him alone."

When the others filed out of the office, the young Mexican entered. He was slight of build, arrow-straight, looked both capable and confident, and had a disarming smile which he flashed at Mike as he removed his hat. In spite of inherent prejudice, Mike liked what he saw. He motioned the youth to a chair.

"The fiesta leaders want you deputised. You know that?"

"I know. They asked me to do this. I agreed, only if you wish it so."

"What's your name?"

"Tomas Velarde, Sheriff."

"Tom, huh?"

The warm smile flashed outwards again. "*Si;* Tom."

"That gun you're wearing, Tom . . ."

Velarde touched the holster with dark, long fingers, desert-coloured and wiry. "I have used it, Sheriff; I have much practise—but I am not so good as you."

Mike drummed on the desk. After a moment of silence he got up. "Stand up, Tom, and raise your right hand." After he had given the younger man the oath, he rummaged for a star-in-a-circlet like he wore, and held it out. As Tom took the badge, Sheriff Mike said, "Now listen, boy; the first swagger I see—the first time you pick a fight—you're fired. You understand?"

"I understand."

"And you take orders only from me. Not from the fiesta *aficionados,* not from the Vacaville town council—just me."

"Just you." The dark eyes were steady. In them lay a blending of pride and respect. "I will obey."

"Fine. Now go on home. I'll look you up in the morning."

"*Buenas noches.*"

After Deputy Tomas Velarde's departure, Mike went to the stove, swished the coffeepot, found that it held only dregs, put it down with a mild oath, took up his hat and went outside. Four doors north was *Hatfield's Cafe.* He seldom patronised it because Amos Hatfield was both a gossip and, in a small way, a trouble-maker; but tonight he could not dredge up the amiability his presence at either saloon invariably required; and besides, all he wanted was a nightcap of coffee.

Inside the cafe, which was nearly empty, Mike sank down on the bench and leaned tiredly upon the counter. Fat, sly-faced Amos Hatfield, talking to a slight, dark-haired man who was smoking at the far end of the counter, came forward with an anticipatory smile.

" 'Evening, Sheriff. Steak and onions—or just coffee."

"Coffee'll be fine."

"Sure." As Hatfield turned toward the pot, he spoke over his shoulder. "Sure was a fine funeral today. Too bad you missed it. Folks really give young Reed a send-off."

"So I heard."

"Yeah," Hatfield said, turning with the cup in his hand. "I hope they do as good for Buel."

Sheriff Mike looked up, into Hatfield's face, and said nothing.

The dark-haired man down the counter spoke up. There was a cocky lilt to his voice which matched the direct brightness of his eyes. "Reed sure has a lot of friends, Sheriff. That procession was from one end of town to the other."

Mike sipped coffee quietly, making no reply. When he put the cup down and reached for his tobacco sack, Amos Hatfield's voice broke into his thoughts.

"Folks had about enough of them Skull Valleyers."

The dark-haired man edged around on the bench. "All it'll take is another killing, I think."

"Then what?" Mike asked quietly.

"Why; then all hell'll bust loose."

"Fred," the sheriff said tiredly. "You're a pretty good saddlemaker. Why don't you stick to that?"

25

The dark-haired man's face flushed with colour and his gaze remained steadfastly on McMahon's profile. "I mind my business, Sheriff," he said quickly, antagonism in each word. "I also keep my ear to the ground. If I was you I'd do the same."

"Why?"

"Why? Why, because if you don't, something's going to explode under that chair of yours one of these days, and you won't know anythin' about it till it's too late."

Sheriff Mike arose, dropped a coin on the counter and turned toward the door, cigarette dangling from his lips. "When that day comes," he said to the saddlemaker, "I'll trade jobs with you, Nolan."

He left the cafe, feeling as irritated as he had known he would feel before he went in. Northward the gloomy jaws of the mountains lay soft-shining in the moonlight. It had been a hot day and the windless night air was warmer than it had been the night before. All in the glowing distance was the smoky outline of peaks and buttes rising upwards from the flat plain, black summits straining toward the heavens.

Mike went home. Doctor Pat was there, still wearing the rusty black suit he'd donned for the funeral. He was reading a thick book and beside his chair was a water-glass of liquor. He looked up as Mike entered, and nodded. "Pretty hot day for riding, wasn't it?" he said.

"Pretty hot all right."

"The funeral went off fine."

"So I've been told."

"Toni looks good in black."

"She looks good in anything," Mike said, sitting down

26

and tugging off his boots. "How was she today?"

"No different. What did you expect?"

"Well," the sheriff said, looking hard at the tall glass of whiskey, "last night I figured you weren't yourself."

"I told you I wasn't drunk."

"Yeah. You've told me that before—then you've gone blundering off like a horse with blind-staggers."

"When I make a diagnosis, it's right—drunk *or* sober." Pat closed the book in his lap with a sharp slap of pages. He watched his brother shake out of his shirt and scratch his ribs. "I'm not as phlegmatic as you are, Mike."

"Is that what I am?" the sheriff asked, getting heavily to his feet. "Maybe it's a good thing, because I can't afford to buy as much whiskey as you do. I used to wonder why in hell anyone'd want to be a sawbones—now I know. Money." He gathered up his clothing and went out of the room. Doctor Pat watched him go, and when the soft pad of footfalls faded, he took up the glass, tilted it far back and drained it.

The next morning Vacaville came to life with an air of expectancy, of anticipation. Before Mike got to the office, people were threading their way toward the Mexican part of town. It was too early for riders from the outlying ranches to arrive yet, but it was not too early for the children to be out, trailed by raffish dogs, shrill barks and shrill voices blending in the hot early light.

Mike was finishing with the mail when the doctor came in. He closed the door and shook his head. "It's going to be a scorcher today."

"Early summer like this means drought later on," Mike said, clearing the table and arising. "To you I guess that means nothing more'n the usual rash of late babies; to me it means short tempers."

"Mike; I'm going to take Toni to the fiesta." Pat's eyes were round and waiting.

The sheriff nodded matter-of-factly. "Sure; will she go?"

"I don't know. But she should."

"Well now, Pat; aren't you rushing things a mite? Reed's only been buried one day. Folks'll talk if she goes, you know."

The doctor snapped his fingers. "Yes, I know. Amos Hatfield and Fred Nolan. But she's got to be snapped out of this. It's therapy, really."

Mike looked at his brother with an ironic expression. "I wish I knew words like that when I want to talk a beautiful girl into going out with me."

"Mike, I'm serious. Every day she broods will make it harder for her to come out of it."

"Let me make a suggestion," the sheriff said. "Take her tonight, when it's dark. Not so many folks'll see her then. That is, if she'll go."

The doctor considered this for a moment, head down and brows knit, then his face cleared and he nodded. "That's good advice. Every once in a while you come up with something intelligent; it surprises me."

Mike grinned. "It surprises me, too." He reached for his hat and started forward. "Well; my work's cut out for me today, Pat. See you later."

They left the office side by side, and for a while they walked together, then the doctor split off bound for his office, and Sheriff Mike continued on through the rising heat toward Mexican-town, the original and older section of Vacaville, where the annual *Fiesta Soldados*—soldier's feast—was celebrated each year, to commemorate the arrival of Spanish troops two hundred years earlier. The troops had lifted a siege by Apache Indians and had saved the populace from massacre, and in true Spanish—and Mexican—style, grateful descendents celebrated the delivery of their ancestors each spring, on the exact day that the soldiers had arrived.

Inevitably, the thanks-giving was now only a brief and hasty interlude attended by older people and priests; it was concluded as speedily as possible in the morning so that the real celebration could get under way, and by the time Sheriff McMahon arrived in Mexican-town, the noise, dust, laughter, shrieks, and movement, were bringing to life once again the *Fiesta Soldados*, a day of gaiety and, usually, a time of amiability.

This morning, before the sun was high enough to burn away all the shadows, the casual alleyways which served as streets, always crooked, always lined on both sides with squat and square adobe houses, were as colourful as brilliant Mexican costumes could make them. And, adding to the strictly Mexican scene, strings of hot-peppers hung drying in the sunlight. Dust, ankle-deep, was kicked to life by booted and sandaled feet. Handsome horsemen cantering by reflected beams of light from silver ornamentation. Where the sheriff finally halted, in the soft shadows of a fenceless *jacal,* a sow lay serenely in the mud puddle formed by an overflowing water-trough, grunting pleasurably and watching the people who whirled past. Mike made a cigarette, lit it, and was throwing down the match when a light, brown hand brushed his sleeve. He turned. It was Tomas Velarde, somberly dressed and with his belt-gun tied down efficiently, but from whose glistening face radiated excitement and pleasure. The sheriff nodded.

"Any trouble?"

"No trouble, *Señor.*" A slight gesture and a smile, wry and knowing. "But it is too early yet for that."

Mike nodded and turned back to watching the throngs. He and Tom Velarde stood slightly apart, silent, relaxed, breathing deeply of the fragrance coming from the barbecue pits where halfs of beeves were cooking under sweaty and watchful Mexican eyes. "There are men from Skull Valley here," the deputy said, finally, jutting ahead with his chin. "There."

Mike saw them and recognised Porter Buel. He could feel his body stiffening unconsciously. Beyond the Skull Valley riders were other horsemen; among them some that Sheriff Mike did not recognise: strangers. He studied each one separately, ticking off faces in his mind, seeking to match them to wanted posters.

"It is hot, no?"

"It's getting hot all right," Mike said, still looking at faces.

"Epifanio Alvarado brought Sonora lemons. I will get us some cold juice."

Mike watched the lithe body move away from him. He thought of other lithe Mexicans he had known, mostly older than Tomas, mostly raiders from south of the line. A deep voice cut across his awareness speaking his name.

"Mike; you're down here early."

"Hello, Hugh. You're out kind of early yourself, aren't you?"

Grant moved into the shade and mopped his face. "Summer's here. Never saw a country could beat this one for sudden heat." The forge owner cocked a look at the sheriff. "Saw a strange thing last night, Mike. Antonia Parker comin' out of the alley near Fifth Street. All alone, at that."

"No harm in that, is there?"

"Noooo," Grant said, drawing the word out. "Mebbe not. Only she ain't the alley-cat kind. 'Specially with young Reed gettin' cold at Pat's office. Seems to me she'd be home cryin'."

Deputy Velarde returned with two tin cups. When he saw Hugh Grant he hesitated, then offered his own cup to the blacksmith. His disappointment vanished when Grant waved the cup aside with a brusque, "No thanks." Then Grant's eyes fell to the badge on Velarde's shirtfront and lifted slowly to Mike's face. The sheriff's glance was wide and unwavering. Grant made a grunt of disapproval and moved off. The crowd swallowed him up, bore him along out of sight.

"This is pretty good stuff," Mike said to Tomas. "Not too sweet like most folks make it."

"Too much sweet, you get thirsty again too soon."

A faint breeze stirred, wafting the scent of the mud puddle to them. Tomas looked apologetic when Mike wrinkled his nose and started to move farther away in the shadows. The restless froth of talk, Spanish and English, followed them. As Mike was facing around again, leaning back, Tomas, who was holding his cup inches from his lips, spoke.

"A stranger, Sheriff. There. That man with the big black horse."

31

Mike looked, and understood his deputy's quick interest. The stranger was young. His face was sun darkened. He wore a dust-powdered dark hat thumbed far back, and from moving, pale eyes, he sat the saddle looking out and over the people. There was no smile on his lips, but just behind his face lay something akin to a smile. A quiet, confident, knowing look; nearly insolent. The stranger wore a tied-down gun in a shiny leather holster, and the way the gun tilted forward a little, the way the stranger's fingers hung unconsciously close to it, even in the saddle, said 'gunman.'

Mike finished cataloguing the stranger and nodded. "Yep. A real hell-fire outlander, Tomas. It'll pay to watch this one."

The stranger caught their stares, and seemed to grow straighter in the saddle although he did not move. Then he nudged the black horse and rode past.

"Shall I watch him?" Tomas asked.

"No. It's pretty early for trouble yet, like you said. We'll look after him later."

The morning passed. A heat-haze came down from the yonder hills and spread over the town. People became listless and many, after eating their fill, sought shade and slept. Mike sauntered back uptown, leaving Tomas at the Fiesta area. He went to the liverybarn. Hank Hubbel was in the office when the sheriff entered. He leaned back in Reed Benton's chair and locked hands behind his head.

"Howdy, Sheriff. 'Want your horse?"

"No; just some answers, Hank."

"Sure. Sit down—relax."

Mike remained standing. "Where did you ride to the other night after you talked to Antonia Parker?"

"Ride to? Me? You got me mixed up with someone else, Sheriff."

"Yeah; of course. Now tell me you didn't meet Antonia, and make a real good lie out of it."

Hubbel's hands came down slowly. His face hardened. "What makes you think I got to lie to you—or anyone like you?"

The sheriff spread his legs. His expression of patience and fatalism thinned a little. The grey-level eyes didn't waver. "You're lyin' Hank, and we both know it. I want to know where you went—what you had in mind doing."

"I didn't ride nowhere."

"And you didn't talk to Miz' Parker."

"Toni?" Hubbel said, mouthing the name slowly. "Yeh; I talked to her. Every once in a while I talk to her. Maybe more now'n before, with Reed gone. That ain't against the law, is it?"

Sheriff Mike felt the hot gush of anger steal upwards into his face. He turned abruptly and left the office. Part way down the barn's wide alleyway, an old man was pushing a wheel-barrow from which arose a strong scent of ammonia. Mike went to him and the old man stopped, looking around.

"Howdy, Sheriff."

"Howdy, G.B. Did a young feller ride in here a while back on a big black horse?"

"Sure did, Sheriff. That's the critter over there in number six. Nice animal; cost someone a pile of money." The hostler's head came back around. "Gunman, ain't he?"

"Is he?"

"C'mon, Sheriff; in this business you get so's you can

spot 'em as easy as in your business."

"How so, G.B.?"

"Well; to start with, they always pay extra for grain and a rub-down—like they might want to ride out on a strong horse in a hurry. Another thing—they always want to know which stall the critter'll be in, and they don't want him moved 'less they're told. Then of course, there's looks; you know what I mean: The look in the face, around the eyes; clothes, gun; like that."

"I guess you're right at that," Mike murmured, and crossed to the stall. "Fine animal all right. I see you've grained him, G.B."

"For a 'dobe dollar I'll damn near founder him, Sheriff." The hostler picked up his wheel-barrow and started forward. He made a detour so as to come close to Mike. In a husked whisper he said, "He talked to Hank a spell, then went hunting."

"Who?"

"Port Buel."

"Thanks."

The hostler went on down the gloomy alleyway and Mike cast a final glance at the black horse. He noted the graceful tracery of a Mexican brand, and, coupling that with what the hostler had said about being given a 'dobe dollar, he knew the gunman was up out of Mexico.

When Mike walked back out into the sunlight, Hank Hubbel craned his neck to watch him go. Then he smiled, and went back to the ledgers he was working over.

The people drifting both ways impeded Sheriff Mike's progress somewhat, and he had just found his deputy when he heard the first shot, dull, flat, and echoing. A second later there was a second shot, muffled sounding. He started forward in a run, Tomas beside him, and when they came to where there was no crowd, and one man lay flat in the mica-sparkling dust, Mike looked across the distance into the nearly-smiling face of the young gunman. He knelt and felt for heartbeat; there was none. He rolled Porter Buel over. A look of surprise was frozen in place upon the dead man's face. Feet shuffled up behind him. Mike arose and turned, three Skull Valley riders were staring from the corpse to the gunman and back down again. A fourth rider was hurrying up; he too, looked disbelieving. Mike cast a significant stare at Tomas and moved across the distance toward the gunman.

"Well, stranger—let's hear your side of it."

Pale, depthless eyes looked hard into the sheriff's face; attentive, ruthless eyes. "Sure, Sheriff; he was pushin' me around over at the barbecue pits. I moved off. He came over by the lemonade barrel and started talkin' big. I called him—and there he is."

"What's your name, mister?"

"Shiloh Smith." The pale eyes flickered. "My pappy was killed at Shiloh durin' the war." A shrug. "Smith—it's as good as Jones, I figure."

Mike turned on the balls of his feet. Over by the lemonade barrel saddlemaker Fred Nolan, and Epifanio Chavez, were standing. The latter was rooted, grey-faced and ill looking. When his eyes raised from the corpse to Mike's face, he said, "It is as I said. Sheriff. Trouble."

"What happened?"

The Mexican continued to stare and say nothing. Mike looked at the saddlemaker. Nolan flicked a quick look at the motionless gunman and looked away. "Like he said. Port choused him—he called him—and Port's gun went off when he was falling." Nolan looked longer at the gunman. "I never saw a draw like it, Mike. His gun was back in the holster when Port hit the ground."

Mike looked farther back. People were eyeing the gunman and shaking their heads to indicate they had seen nothing. Mike called for other witnesses; there were none. He turned back to Shiloh Smith.

"All right, mister; you come with me."

Smith stepped back. "What for? You heard what that feller said. It was self-defence."

"Just the same we've got laws here. I'll take your deposition for the circuit judge when he gets to town. Too bad you didn't do this yesterday; the judge was still here."

Smith loosened; he made a small grin. "All right." He started forward, saw the four Skull Valley riders watching him with coldness on their faces, and halted. "You fellers his friends? Well; I'll be around," he said, then went past, keeping stride with Sheriff Mike.

People moved back, some muttered as the sheriff and Shiloh Smith went by. At the beginning of the plankwalk Sheriff Mike met Will Herman, nightbarman at *Householder's Saloon*. He asked him to see that the body of Porter Buel was delivered to Doctor Pat's office. As the lawman and gunman walked on, Herman's mouth dropped open and stayed that way until Mike pushed open his office door and flagged Smith inside.

The office was cool and pleasant. Mike went behind the table and sat down. He motioned for Smith to go back against the wall and sit on the bench. Then he took up a pencil and smoothed out a sheet of blank paper and began the questions. When the recitation was finished and Shiloh Smith had signed it, Sheriff Mike tossed aside the pencil and looked steadily at the gunman.

"Why, Smith?"

The pale eyes showed hard humour. "You've got it all down there in black and white, Sheriff. What more d'you want?"

"The rest of it."

Smith's bleak grin began to fade. "What the hell are you talking about?"

"You rode up here from Mexico. It's a long, dusty ride. You came because you were sent for. I'm pretty sure I know who got you to come to Vacaville. What I want to know now is—if I'm right or not—and how much you got for killing Porter Buel."

"Like I already told you—this feller was a stranger to me; he kept chousin' me, so I called him. He was pretty cocky and now he's dead. That's the whole story."

Sheriff Mike shook his head. "No it isn't. Tell me, Smith—who do you know in Vacaville?"

"No one. I was just passin' through. I saw the fiesta goin' on and figured I'd stop for a few hours."

"Passing through out of Mexico?"

"Sure; lots of folks live in Mexico who aren't Mexicans."

"Where were you headed?"

"Up north. Colorado, maybe, or Wyoming. Spring round-up time you know." Smith stood up. His expression was edged with antagonism now. He hooked both thumbs in his shell-belt and looked steadily into the sheriff's face. "I'm supposed to meet some friends of mine at Junction

City, east of here. If I'm not there—they'll be down here lookin' for me. You wouldn't like that, Sheriff." He moved toward the door, put a hand on the latch, and lifted. "Anyway; from what I've heard Buel's no loss. You ought to thank me."

"A stranger wouldn't hear anything that quick," McMahon said, getting to his feet.

"All right; maybe I heard about Buel somewhere else. What's the difference; he's dead. Now you don't have to worry about him killin' any more upstandin' citizens. Adios, Sheriff." Smith opened the door and passed through.

Mike moved around the corner of the table and was half way to the door when the shot came, flat and vicious sounding. Mike wrenched the door wide and passed through, then stopped. Shiloh Smith was lying half on, half off, the plankwalk. As the sheriff watched, he pushed himself upwards with great, straining effort, and tried to raise his head. He couldn't; his head swung from side to side, then fell forward. Smith's arms buckled and went flat, dust spurting up around him.

The sheriff stood wide-legged squinting into the shimmering nearness of Vacaville's long main thoroughfare. There were people, mostly frozen in motion by the sound of the shot, but there was no one in sight carrying a naked gun. As Mike bent, raised Shiloh Smith and looked briefly into his face, the door of *Hatfield's Cafe* slammed closed and a man's hard footfalls jarred forward. Mike let the dead man down and drew up straight.

"Mike!"

"Howdy, Pat. Don't bother feeling around; he's dead.

Right through the chest."

The doctor bent anyway, and rolled the gunman over, hunched closer to study the wound, then drew back for a look at the stilled face, before he got up and dusted his knees. He spoke without turning toward his brother.

"Is he the one who shot Buel?"

"Yes. Called himself Shiloh Smith."

Doctor Pat looked long and searchingly across the roadway. "Who did it. That shot came from a distance, Mike."

"Likely we'll never know."

Pat whirled. His eyes came up short against the unblinking stare of the sheriff. "Whoever did it, Mike, is a murderer."

"Sure is."

"It's your job to find him and hold him for trial."

"Sure is."

"Then *do* it—don't just stand there like a damned wooden Indian!"

Mike McMahon's nostrils pinched down against an out-going breath. "You get some boys to cart him down to your embalming shed, Pat," he said in a mild voice. "And you get the usual stuff from his pockets, and notify the next-of-kin—if any—then you have him planted decent-like, and go get a stiff drink, and leave the rest to me, will you?"

Doctor Pat's face blanched, his dark-ringed eyes grew large and hot looking, then he whirled and walked swiftly away, outrage in every line of his back.

"Sheriff . . . ?"

Mike turned. "Hello, Tom. How're things down at the fiesta?"

Velarde stared long at the sun-brightened corpse. "Who did it?" he whispered.

"That's not hard to figure out," Mike said, turning away. "Come on inside; I've got a little job for you."

CHAPTER THREE

DURING THE HALF-LIGHT, half-dark hour following sunset when a soft quiet lay over Vacaville while people ate and rested, and before they went back to the fiesta for the night's entertainment, a solitary horseman loped out of town, bending northeasterly. It was Tomas Velarde, and Sheriff McMahon watched him go, knowing his messenger wouldn't get to Junction City until midnight or later. When the sound of the horse died away, the sheriff started down toward Mexican-town. A few strollers were ahead of him, but not many. The evening was cool and pleasant. As he passed *Householder's Saloon* several dusty riders clattered up and swung down with a whoop. He eyed them briefly and passed on.

Mexican-town, too, was catching its second breath. Candlelight gleamed from doorways and lilting Spanish, softly musical in the afterglow of dying day, was pleasing to hear. Beyond the plaza where the severely plain adobe church stood, vesper bells rang, and a number of older people walked in that direction.

Gradually, as darkness came down and the mystery of an Arizona night closed in, the strollers became more numerous, and an hour later, the crowd was surging again, its voice a loud, insistent hum. Sheriff Mike allowed himself to be herded along, from the barbecue pits to the puppet shows, and finally, to the cleared place where Mexican players from Chihuahua would give a rendition of an old Spanish drama, probably a tragedy, since, as far back as Mike McMahon could remember, that was the type of play enacted at all *Fiestas Soldados*; gloomy, sad stories of unrequited love, usually with either the hero or heroine plunging a dagger into their breast at the finale. Then he glimpsed his brother and Antonia Parker, and every thought was swept from his mind so that his attention could close down around them.

He had not believed the girl would attend the fiesta, and even now, as they came toward him through the press of bodies, he sought for reluctance in her expression. There was none; in fact there was no expression at all. Her face was pale and impassive, the full lips lying closed but without pressure, the beautiful eyes steady and unseeing.

Mike moved anglingly to intercept them. Doctor Pat saw him and stopped. Antonia looked up, and for a second there was swift intentness in her glance, then it faded and the lovely eyes were empty again.

"Glad to see that you're out, Toni," the sheriff said, and flicked a short nod to his brother.

Doctor Pat, catching a glimpse of Fred Nolan in the crowd, half turned, holding the girl's arm out. "Mike," he said, "walk with her a while. I've got to see Nolan—he's making me a new harness for the dental chair."

Mike felt uncomfortable, looking down at the girl. The last time they had talked it had been unpleasant. He took her arm and steered her through the crowd, aware of the quick stares around them. Then Antonia drew her arm away and the silence between them became thicker. Finally, Mike edged her out of the crowd and toward a bench that stood vacant in the dark shadows of a Mexican house. They sat down. Mike was conscious of the fragrance of her hair and the closeness of her body.

"Toni," he said quietly, "are you satisfied now? Have you got all the bitterness out of your heart?"

She didn't answer him directly, although she raised her face and the rising moon threw soft light across it, showing the strong, durable beauty there. "Why did you ask that, Sheriff? Do you know something?"

He nodded without speaking and her eyes searched his face.

"What do you know?"

"I think I know what's on your conscience."

"All of it?"

"I believe so; yes."

She looked away. "You couldn't—not all of it."

"Do you want me to tell you?"

"Yes."

"You sent Hank Hubbel to hire a fast gun to kill Porter Buel. He came—calling himself Shiloh Smith—and he killed Port, and you felt avenged. Then, this afternoon, some of Port's friends from Skull Valley killed Smith. And now you're a little sick about it."

She threw him a startled look and lowered her head, but not before he had seen dark, unknown things lying in her eyes.

"Am I right?" he asked.

"Yes."

Mike settled back loosely and spoke impersonally,

without looking at her. "But that isn't all of it, Toni. Smith has friends over at Junction City. Friends who'll want to avenge him just like Buel's friends from the Valley avenged him. So you see, when you draw a gun—or hire one to be drawn—you don't get revenge so much as you insure other killings." He said this quietly, as though it didn't matter greatly, and Toni, looking askance at his face, saw something there she had never seen before; fatalism. She locked her hands together in her lap and looked at the ground in front of her.

"I'm sorry. What can I do? I wasn't myself. I loved Reed."

Mike moved slightly on the bench, as though something pained him, then he said, "I can't tell you it's all right; to forget it; because you'll never forget it and it isn't all right."

"You knew Reed. He spoke of you and Doctor Pat often."

"We grew up together, just like we grew up with you, Toni, and half the other people in Vacaville." He shot her a long, still glance. "You were the most beautiful girl in town, in those days. I reckon every kid in Vacaville's been in love with you one time or another. We admired you, too."

Her head came up and turned, and her gaze was steady now. "You don't admire me now, Mike?"

"No."

They grew silent, and distantly someone struck a drum so that its deep-booming echo rolled outwards in shock-waves. The people began moving toward the cleared space; cowboys with their girls, Mexican lasses—faces ghostly white with flour-paste cosmetic—and their swarthy escorts; older people, Mexicans and American, more anxious to sit down than to see the play. Over it all, struggling against impossible odds, a Mexican orchestra of guitars, flutes and drums, strove to beat down the loud hum of talk.

A fat Mexican came by the bench where they sat, carrying a smoky tar-torch. With an apologetic smile and shrug he stuck it into a wall holder and passed on. The hot, hard light twisted and jerked, casting macabre shadows at their feet. Mike blinked upwards at the torch and leaned forward.

"Walk with me," he said.

Antonia dutifully arose, took his arm and passed deeper into the shadows, away from the direction most people were taking. At a little booth he bought them both a cup of bitter chocolate. They drank in silence and moved still farther away from the noise of the fiesta. Finally, Mike stopped and half turned to face her, and Toni drew up also, her face pale and composed in the moonlight.

"I reckon we all live and learn," he said. "Today you've had your chance."

Her hands moved in a slight, helpless gesture. "What can I do?"

"Nothing. Ride out the storm like I'm going to do. 'Isn't so bad to make a mistake, Toni; it's only bad when you repeat it."

"But—what will happen?"

"That's what I'm trying to anticipate. I sent a man to Junction City to check on Smith's friends. Tomorrow, I'm going down to Skull Valley. If there's a war shaping up, I aim to nip it in the bud. If I'm successful, you'll have learnt something, and all I'll be out is a little time." He started to resume their walk but she did not move.

"It's a terrible thing to love someone."

He halted and looked at her, hard. "Did you, Toni? Did you really love him that much?"

She heard the strangeness in his voice and was briefly puzzled by it. "What do you mean—did I love him that much?"

"Just what I said. I've known you a long time. I've seen you with other men before Reed."

"But—of course you have. At the dances and socials and all—but that was different. I can tell you—"

"No; don't," Mike said quickly. "Come on; I'll walk you home."

They went silently down through the crooked lanes of Mexican-town, and finally, through the moonlighted emptiness of Vacaville's Front Street. When they turned east on Grant Street, Antonia looked sideways at him several times, and slowed her steps until they stopped altogether at her front gate.

"Mike; I apologise for the way I acted the other night. I'm ashamed of myself. I know you better than to think you're a coward—that you were indifferent about the killing."

"I could understand that, all right," he answered, groping for his tobacco sack and lowering his eyes to make a cigarette. "I expect I understood about the other, too—only understanding doesn't change anything."

"No; of course it doesn't." She watched his face glow shortly under the match's flame, then dim out into shadow again, and she heard the long sweep of breath as he exhaled. "Mike; this is very odd."

"What is?" His grey-level eyes were on her face unwaveringly.

"This—us—tonight. I've seen you, well, for years. Before my parents died, they knew your parents. I—but I never really knew you before."

"Well," he said slowly, "I got out of school a couple of years ahead of you. I guess I was too old to run with the kids you knew."

She shook her head, watching his face. "No; I don't think that's it. At least not all of it. It's just that you've always been, well, withdrawn. We've never even danced together. And tonight, at the fiesta, that was the first time I've ever actually walked with you—in the moonlight."

He looked down at the cigarette in his fingers. "And that wasn't exactly pleasant, was it?"

She watched smoke riffle straight up in the bland, still night, from his cigarette, and her voice came softly in a murmur. "Yes; it was pleasant, Mike—the last part of it." Then she took a step closer to him, with soberness in her face, holding it dark and still, and she held up a hand. He took it, still not looking into her face, and pressed her palm with his fingers, and the stillness ran on, full of puzzling emotions and unexpressed thoughts, until she withdrew the hand. Then he cast down the cigarette and stepped on it, grinding down hard with his heel.

She saw the graceful sweep of hatbrim, the black cut of his shoulders, and knew, even though she could not see his face, that it was set in a hard way, the lips drawn back, the eyes full of movement. Then his hands came up, touched her arms, moved up higher, brushed the fullness of her briefly, and settled tightly near the shoulders, with forward pressure. She lifted her head to meet his face and put both hands upon his chest without pressure, and that was the way she stood when their lips met; when the full shock of his hunger engulfed her, burning deep, making her feel weak before his will. Then he moved back, looking into her eyes. For a moment they were still and silent, then he took her arm, steered her beyond the gate to the porch and stopped at the door.

"Good night, Toni."

"Good night, Mike."

He heard the door latch fall into place, then went back to the dust of Grant Street, and started heavily toward the yonder plankwalk. When he hit it, boots making deep sounds upon the wood, he was heading toward *Householder's Saloon*, and he was still there, sitting loose and dry-eyed with an untouched onion sandwich and a partially drained glass of beer an hour later, when Doctor Pat came in for a nightcap, paused, stared at his brother, then went to the table and drew up a chair, frowning.

"Wher'd you disappear to?"

"We walked like you said, then I took her home."

Pat's eyes drew out narrow. "What's wrong with you; feel all right?"

Mike's gaze lowered to his brother's face and focused only gradually. "I think I feel all right," he said. "I'm not just sure."

"What kind of an answer is that?" Pat got up. "Wait; I'll get a bottle."

Mike did not move, not even after Pat had returned, dropped down with a loud sigh, and drank thirstily, set the glass aside and resumed his study of the sheriff's face. "Now; tell me your symptoms."

"I don't have any. Just confusion, Pat."

The doctor's look sharpened. "Toni?"

"Yeah. Tell me, Pat—what you said about her the other night—about that insanity business—how long will it last?"

"I see what's troubling you, now. She seemed normal tonight, didn't she?"

"I think she did. I hope she did, Pat."

"Well; she is normal. The thing is, Mike, Buel's killing had the effect of a great shock on her. It snapped her back to rationality—just like that." Pat snapped his fingers, then his gaze clouded. "But why Buel should have such an effect I can't say. The human mind's a strange—"

"Want me to tell you?"

"What? Tell me what?"

"About Buel's effect on Toni."

Pat leaned on the table. "Can you?" he asked.

"Sure. She sent Hubbel to hire Smith to come here and kill Buel."

The doctor leaned back and stared. "No . . ." He said. "I don't believe it . . . Because of Reed?"

The sheriff nodded, seeing the horror on his brother's face. "Sure; what's so unusual about revenge?"

"But *Toni,* Mike."

"She's human, too."

Pat began to wag his head. "I'm disillusioned," he mumbled, reaching for the glass beside him. "I'm completely disillusioned." He drank deeply and put the glass down, but did not relinquish his hold on it. "Toni . . ."

"Pat," the sheriff said softly, "sometimes I can't figure you out. Last night you were worrying because she was so upset over Reed's death. You were afraid it'd leave her deranged. Now, tonight, because something else snapped her back to normal—you're even more upset."

"But what a monstrous thing for her to do."

Mike's gaze grew ironic. "Isn't that exactly what you were hoping would happen to Buel? Isn't that what two-thirds of Vacaville wanted to happen to him?"

"That isn't the point, though."

Mike got up and yawned. "Sure it is, Pat. You couldn't expect Toni to go up against Port with a gun—she did the next thing to pop into her mind. And Pat—if, like you say, your diagnoses are never wrong—drunk or sober—she was half-crazy with grief when she did it."

The doctor looked up, wonderingly, at his brother. "Why are you defending her like this—in what amounts to murder?"

The sheriff started to reply when the tinkle of spur rowells over by the door distracted him. When he saw the lithe, dark shadow crossing towards him, he stiffened and a slow frown settled over his face. He turned, with his back to the doctor, and said, "Tom; you couldn't have made it to Junction City and back in this time—what happened?"

The deputy's face was lightened by alkali dust, as was his clothing. "I didn't have to go all the way, Sheriff. I met four riders near Banjan Wells, this side of the river. They asked me about Vacaville." One hand flagged backwards, toward the night. "They are coming here—Smith's friends."

"How do you know they're his friends?"

"They told me, *Señor.* They asked first of the town; then

49

they asked me of him—of Shiloh Smith. I told them only that, yes, I knew of him. They said he was to meet them last night and he had not done so, they were coming after him." Velarde's face screwed up into an expression of anxiety. "They are hard men, Sheriff—*mala hombres*—bad men."

Doctor Pat, who had been listening, got to his feet. "What is it, Mike?" Some of Velarde's anxiety had been transmitted to Pat. "What men—who are they?"

"Shiloh Smith's running mates. He said they'd come here if he didn't meet them at Junction City."

"Does that mean trouble, Mike?"

The sheriff looked at his brother with a smile that moved no farther up his face than his lips, and he replied laconically. "The fiesta ended tonight; I don't think they're coming to town for that. Go on home, Pat. I'll be along directly."

"But if they're—"

"Forget it, will you? They can't stir up much trouble tonight. Tomorrow will be another day."

After his brother had left, Sheriff Mike ordered a beer and sandwich for Tomas Velarde and resumed his place at the table. While the deputy was eating, he answered questions. Finally, Sheriff Mike just sat there, looking at nothing, and when his deputy finished wolfing down the food, he too relaxed, but with the difference that his liquid dark eyes went to McMahon's face and stayed there.

"They will be coming soon," Velarde said.

Mike roused himself and stood up from the table for the second time. "Yeah; well; there's no point in waiting up for them. See you in the morning, Tom. Good night."

"*Buenas noches, jefe; hasta mañana.*"

The walk homeward was pleasant, as was the feeling of bed after he got there. For a long time sleep would not come, then, when it seemed that he had just closed his eyes, sunlight was flooding the room, and he arose, only slightly less tired than he had been when he had finally fallen asleep.

Pat was leaving the house when the sheriff entered the parlour. From the doorway the doctor looked back with a grim expression, and when he spoke it was as though there had been no nocturnal interlude to their conversation.

"I'll think of that every time I look at her—every time I see her."

Mike rubbed his jaw imperturbably, squinting across the room. "Pat; they taught you a lot of useful stuff at medical school, I know; but one thing they taught you that's all wrong—is that belief of yours that all life is good—worth saving."

"You don't know what you're saying, Mike."

"Yes I do; it's you that's mixed up: Crying for Buel's blood one minute, and deploring his death the next minute."

"But it was the way—"

"Naw; that isn't it. You either want a man dead or you don't. How he dies isn't the important thing. And Pat—Buel had it coming."

"But Toni—"

"Toni was the logical one to engineer it. You don't know anyone who had a better right, and you know it. Now go deliver a baby, or set a broken leg, or something."

Pat lingered at the door. "Are you going after Smith's friends?"

"Maybe; in time. If they hang around Vacaville, or make

trouble while they're here. Today, though, I'm going over to Skull Valley."

Pat closed the door softly, leaving Mike to finish dressing, get his breakfast, and wrestle with his thoughts. It was half an hour later, when he entered the sheriff's office, that he found Tomas Velarde waiting for him, and after a curt greeting, he stood behind the table looking down at the highly polished badge lying there. Then he looked up.

"Are you quitting—so soon?"

"Quitting? But no—it was only for the fiesta."

Mike wagged his head. "No," he said. "If you want to stay on I'd be proud to have you." He tossed the badge to Tomas and watched him pin it on with a wide, flashing smile, then he sat down, scuffed through the mail, pushed it aside and leaned forward. "Tom; we've got the makings of real trouble. I'm going out to Skull Valley today, and I want you to keep things peaceful here. All right?"

"I will do my best."

"And Tom—about Shiloh Smith's friends—avoid 'em. Understand?"

"Yes, I understand. You think odds of two-to-one are better than four-to-one."

Mike got up with a short laugh. It changed his face when he smiled; made him look younger, less burdened with thoughts and responsibilities. "That's it in a nutshell. I'll be back sometime tonight—with any luck."

He got his horse from the liverybarn and rode south through town and out across the long drop of land, southerly, setting a course parallel to the stage-road, but straighter. Westward was a gentle rising, toward heat-hazed mountains; eastward was open country as far, and farther, than the sheriff could see. Behind him was Vacaville, and farther back, across the breast of range, the Mogollons, the Pinals, and the Tortilla Mountains. Southward, the way he was riding, lay Skull Valley, and beyond it, a distant blur, were more mountains. Fine alkali dust jerked to life under his horse and hours later, both McMahon and his mount were covered by it.

At Casadora Creek he stopped to water his animal and smoke a cigarette. Farther on, where the road to Banjan Wells intersected the Vacaville Road, he stopped again, and by then it was almost mid-day, with a pale, relentless sun burning downwards. He considered it from the shade of a scraggly cottonwood tree and thought how it would burn in another month, when summer really hit the desert.

Casadora Creek was the mythical boundary line of Skull Valley. From there on, the land was gravelly and shallow, tufted by sparse clumps of buffalo grass, interspersed with hair-like forage-grass, and infrequently, by common varieties of cacti. It was a deadly waste in mid-summer, but now, with green showing, it was only a little forbidding.

For years, in fact since before the Mexican War brought the Arizona Territory to the Union, Skull Valley had been notorious for its elusive travellers, and for its root-down settlers. Because people shunned it, outlaws and renegades of every stripe had rested there. Many had remained; had married into the Mexican families there and raised up broods of hard-riding, hard-fighting, hard-thinking generations. Like wolves, the people of Skull Valley were close and clanny. Their dislike of strangers was only second to their dislike of the law, and if the name of their territory did not discourage wayfarers, its isolation usually did. But, in fact, Skull Valley did not derive its name from relics left from Apache days; the name came from a huge skull of a prehistoric beast which was embedded in stone near the southernmost road into and out of the area, on the California Road.

Where the sheriff rode, following wagon ruts through blanched soil as grey and lifeless as death, a traveller could look outwards and downwards a little, and see distant spots of thick greenery and shade; those were the ranches, scattered far out and appearing as gloomy specks cast down in immensity. It was a big land. A big, hushed land; a place of many secrets, and it was inevitable that some of the hard-riding cowmen, out checking cattle-drift, should sight him; ride closer for a second, confirming look, then send men fanning out to carry the word of his coming.

Nor was Mike surprised when he rode into the yard of the Pratlys, to find the whole clan there on the porch, waiting for him, sitting idly slack and comfortable. He dismounted, gave his reins to a lad sent to care for his horse, and moved up into the shade. George and Jess Pratly, brothers, elderly men of granite mien and few words, acknowledged his nod, and George, the youngest, closed his clasp-knife with slow finality, pocketed it, and waited. The silence was thunderous loud.

"I reckon you've all heard what happened in town yesterday," Mike said, pacing his words to the mood of the people around him.

George Pratly nodded shortly. "Yep; we heard. Fancy gunslinger got hisself salted down f'killin' Port Buel." Another brusque headshake. "'T'waren't no more'n he had coming."

"Maybe not," Mike said in reply. "But the way he got it was pretty cowardly, George."

The silence drew out, became oppressive and awkward, until Jess Pratly's squeaking, thin voice broke it.

"Shurf; a man protects his own."

"From cover—like an Indian?"

Jess Pratly lapsed into sullen silence. The plain-faced, tired looking women rocked in their chairs looking past the men, out where heat shimmered and the mountains marched down then drew back again; they were all impassively silent, but straining to catch each word.

"Who did it, George?" the sheriff asked.

"Cussed if I know."

"Jess?"

"Dunno."

One of the teen-age girls drew up in her chair. She was in the first blush of womanhood, and blood ran under her cheeks as she spoke. "Riders comin'."

Mike turned, saw the dust spiralling, and leaned against an overhang upright, waiting. When they were close he recognised them with no trouble, Slick Bennett, Pug Feltham, Locke Hibbard, and Jack Arbuckle—the men who had been with Porter Buel at the fiesta. He waited until they were skidding to a halt with dust spewing upwards, then he began making a cigarette, and by the time the men were moving away from their mounts, towards the house, he lit up and exhaled, looking straight at them.

"Howdy, boys."

They acknowledged the greeting with nods. None of them spoke until they were at the porch, then Locke Hibbard—the only one with two guns, tied down, and a good deal of silver on his equipment—greeted the Pratlys first, Sheriff Mike second. The greeting was offhand but the hard stare that accompanied it was not.

"You're a long ways from home, ain't you, Sheriff?"

Mike inclined his head and passed over the remark. "We were just talking about the killings in town yesterday," he said, pushing the words out distinctly. "What I'm interested in, is who shot the gunman?"

Hibbard, as tall but only half as broad as Mike McMahon, slouched in the shade. "Lot of folks in Vacaville yesterday," he said. "Could've been any one of 'em."

"Could've been—only they had no call to bushwhack the gunman."

"Unless you're real fast that's the on'y way to get you a gunman, Sheriff."

"Maybe; but you've got to have a yellow streak down your back a yard wide to do it that way."

Hibbard drew up gradually until he was erect, and colour darkened his face. When he didn't speak George Pratly said, "Now Sheriff—let's not have no trouble. Leastaways not here, in front of the younguns and all."

Mike smoked a moment in silence. Then he crushed out the cigarette and spoke around a streamer of blue smoke. "Who was it, Locke?"

"Can't say right off hand, Sheriff." The tone matched the look, with insolence and dislike.

Mike felt anger growing in him. "All right, boys; now I'm going to pass you a little word of advice. Stay out of Vacaville for the next two weeks."

The elder Pratly, eyes like stone, regarded the lawman from beneath bushy brows. "Are y'tellin' us we can't come to town, Shurf?"

"Yes. Particularly Locke here, and Pug, Slick and Jack."

"You got no right to make no order like that," Pratly said on a rising note. "Who d'you think you are, anyway; the guvnor?"

"Jess; I'm trying to prevent trouble. I aim to do it the only way I can. If some of you older folks have to come to town for supplies, come ahead—but none of these boys like Pug and Jack, and Slick and Locke."

George Pratly was studying Mike's face, now he said, "I expect you got a reason for makin' such a law, Sheriff. What is it? Folks in town het up against us again?" Pratly made a disdaining gesture. "We've met up with that before—we can handle it."

"Not in my town you can't, George. You're just going to wait this out."

"Well now—that ain't no way to settle trouble, is it? Hidin' from it?"

"I'm not trying to settle trouble, George, I'm trying to avoid it."

The craggy-faced rancher got heavily to his feet, eyes squinted against sunblast. "Can't be done," he said emphatically. "I know. I been tryin' to avoid trouble all my life, and it just plain can't b'done." He turned and started across the porch toward the door. His voice changed, became softly brittle and as hard as iron. "I reckon the boys can come to Vacaville if they've a mind to, Sheriff—and as long as they behave theirselves—why I don't see where you'll have call to make trouble for 'em." He disappeared beyond the door, letting it swing closed behind him with a sound of finality.

CHAPTER FOUR

MIKE HAD INTENDED to ride to the other ranches; to Stone Gorman's place, Carl Braun's, and maybe as far south as the ranch of Carlos Fortier, but he knew, as he was riding away from Pratly's that the motionless people back there who were watching him, would carry the word of his coming, and of his words.

He also knew, or felt sure that he knew, who had ambushed Shiloh Smith. He had seen it in Locke Hibbard's face when he had said the man who had done the killing was yellow. But he felt no obligation to arrest Hibbard; if the murdered man had been a merchant, or even a gambler from Dade Carleton's *Casino* or Charley Householder's saloon, he might have attempted it, but Sheriff Mike's philosophy about killers was different from book-law. He had seen too many gunmen come and go to believe it was necessary to arrest them when their killings were confined to shootouts with other gunmen. Experience had taught him that if a gunman was given enough rope, he would eventually find retribution at the hand of another gunman. Like all wise frontier lawmen, he never forced trouble, but waited until it came to him, and by then the odds were usually about even; then he went into action.

He made good time on the return trip and stopped only once, at Casadora Creek. After that he pushed along the stony roadway with fine alkali dust roiling up around him as dry as flour, settling over him, greying his mount, and stinging his eyes. He saw the low blur of Vacaville on the horizon as the sun was turning red and throwing dagger-like streaks of purple far out, upon the mountainsides. Later, as he was plodding up to the outskirts, the sun sank still lower; hung upon a jagged peak like a punctured egg-yolk, flooding the plains with a last gush of scarlet light, then began to sink swiftly from sight.

It was soft-evening when he dismounted at the livery-barn. Vacaville was quiet and lethargic. It was too late for business and too early for the riders to lope in from the ranches. He beat dust from his clothing, cast a glance after his horse, which was being led away by the nighthawk, then he started south toward the office, and at once spied Tom Velarde watching him from in front of *Hatfield's Cafe.* The deputy made a small salute as Mike approached and slowed to a halt. His glance was inquiring.

"Long ride," the sheriff said. "But I may have done a little good. At least I tried, and a man can't do more than deserve a little luck—he can't force it." The grey-level eyes were unmovingly on Tom's face, waiting.

Velarde tipped his hatbrim toward *Carleton's Casino.* "They are in there. They know what happened. It was easy for them to find out; they asked questions and there were many who would tell them."

"Any trouble?"

"No. No trouble. They are sitting at a table. They have been sitting there most of the afternoon. They say nothing except to each other." The dark eyes went to Mike's face. "Do you want to know their names?"

Mike's grin came slowly. Approval lay in his eyes. "Yeah. Come on; let's go look at the flyers. We might find 'em there."

But wanted posters rarely had pictures of outlaws. Descriptions yes, and names, but a name was an easy thing to alter, and descriptions could fit anyone. Mike left Tom leafing hopefully through the pile of flyers and made coffee. When he had poured two cups and given the deputy one of them, he sat down at the table and leaned back.

"Hugh Grant been around?" he asked.

Velarde looked at him curiously. "It is strange that you should ask—yes. Twice today he asked for you."

Mike sipped coffee. "Not so strange, Tom. Y'see, Hugh's chairman of the town council. They make the appropriations for my office. They have never allowed enough money for me to pay a deputy. Hugh saw you at the fiesta wearing a star. I figured he'd be checking to see if you're still wearing it today."

Velarde stacked the flyers very neatly, wearing a thoughtful look. Finally he said, "He doesn't like Mexicans, Sheriff. I saw that yesterday, when he looked at me."

Mike finished the coffee and began making a cigarette. "Nothing unusual about that, Tom. Lots of Mexes don't like *gringos.*"

"That is the truth."

The sheriff's eyes looked out over the cigarette. They were steady and compassionate looking. "I reckon it's up to you to show Grant there are plenty of Mexicans who are as good as *gringos*—just like it's up to me to show your people all *gringo* lawmen aren't gunmen. Right?"

Velarde's solemnity vanished. He made a slow, warm smile. "Right."

"As for the pay—don't worry about it. Hugh's a reasonable man; a little set in his ways, but reasonable." For a moment Mike smoked in silence, listening to the quiet beyond the office door, then he nodded toward the racked guns on the west wall. "Ever handle a riot-gun, Tom?"

"No."

"There's nothing to it. Those four on the wall there— they're loaded with Number Four buckshot. The sawed-off barrels make the shot scatter out in a big, wide pattern. You don't have to aim a riot-gun, just point it in the general direction of whatever you want to hit. But remember this; a sawed-off shotgun's range is short. Don't try to kill with it over a hundred feet; two hundred feet at the outside. You understand?"

"*Si.*"

Sheriff Mike got up, stubbed out his cigarette and settled his hip-holster into place. "Get one of the guns, Tom. Be sure it's loaded, and come with me."

Outside, shadows were lengthening, layer upon layer of them. Sheriff Mike and his deputy crossed through the deserted roadway towards *Carleton's Casino.* As they stepped up onto the plankwalk, Mike stopped and half turned.

"No gunman in his right mind will face a shotgun at close quarters—like in a saloon, Tom. You just stand back by the door and cover Smith's friends. I won't get between you and them, and if any of them goes for his gun—you can cut all four of them in two at that range."

Deputy Velarde licked his lips and nodded. There were beads of sweat along his upper lip. Mike studied him a moment, then slapped him lightly on the shoulder, turned, and pushed through the doors in front of him.

Carleton's Casino was the favourite hangout of Vacaville's rough set. It was also patronised heavily by range riders. Dade Carleton, the owner, was a hard man with a past. He tolerated things which Charley Householder, his competitor, would not stand for, and more than a score of men had died violently in the *Casino*, since Dade Carleton had established it, four years earlier, in the summer of 1884.

Sheriff Mike, who had little use for Dade Carleton, rarely visited the *Casino* unless called there to halt fights or arrest drunks, and when he entered now, with Tom Velarde behind him carrying a riot-gun, the swarthy, scar-faced man behind the bar looked up and froze. Mike threw him a barely perceptible nod and went directly along the bar toward the only occupied table in the room. Four travel-stained men sitting there, looked up at him. They had not missed seeing Tom at the door, with the shotgun, and they, too, were motionless.

The quick hush was broken when Mike spoke, gently and softly. " 'Evening, gents; I'm Sheriff McMahon. You looking for someone, here in Vacaville?"

For a long second no reply came back, then the tall, fair man facing the sheriff, spoke in a dry, clipped way. "Not any more we ain't, Sheriff. We found him. He's yonder in your boothill."

"Shiloh Smith?"

"That's right."

"Well—then I guess you've got no call to hang around, have you?"

The fair man's lips closed in a thin line and he stared at the sheriff without speaking. Another man at the table, a Mexican, loosed a slurred sentence of English.

"We go—when the man who killed him is also dead."

Mike was thoughtfully silent a moment, eyes ranging over the upturned faces before him. Finally he said, "You'd be Belasco, wouldn't you? Dominguez Belasco?"

"*Si;* that's me."

"Which one of you is Curt Slidell?"

The fair man inclined his head slightly without answering.

"And Doughbelly Lowndes?"

A thin man with effeminate features, a cruel mouth, and moving, pale eyes, nodded. Mike looked at the last man, rangy unshaven, with Texan stamped in the height of cheekbones and the long glint of restless eyes.

"Then you'll be Matthew Sheridan?"

"I am."

"All right boys; now we know each other, and friendly-like, I'm telling you to leave Vacaville."

Slidell's steady, glowing eyes clouded over. "We've been mindin' our own business, Sheriff. We aim to go on mindin' it."

"Good; and you can mind it just as well on the trail as you can here in town."

Slidell's milky gaze lingered on Mike. "And what about the feller that bushwhacked Smith? You got him in your 'dobe jailhouse yet?"

"No."

Slidell's stiffness softened slightly. His impassivity lessened to let bleakness show through. "I expect you know that we know who he is."

"Then you know more than I do. Who is he?"

"Feller from down in Skull Valley. Feller by the name of

Jack Arbuckle."

"You're dead wrong, Slidell. It wasn't Jack, I'll stake my life on that."

"This Arbuckle a friend of yours, Sheriff?"

"No."

"You said you didn't know who gunned Smith—how come you to say now it wasn't this Arbuckle feller?"

"Because there's no proof, that's why."

"We got enough proof for us, mister."

"Yeah; talk. Free and easy talk from people who know even less about it than you do."

"That's good enough for us."

"I know that," the sheriff replied, his voice turning hard. "If you kill one—and it's the wrong one—you can always try for another one."

Slidell made a mirthless, small smile. "That's about right," he said. "Now; if it'd been a fair fight, why maybe we wouldn't be choosin' up sides. Or even if the law hereabouts was up and comin'; but it looks to us like folks in Vacaville ain't interested in Shiloh Smith—or how he got it, and Shiloh was a friend of ours. We'll set things to rights."

Mike was standing easy with the bar at his back; he was well to the right of the table and the men seated around it. Tom's riot-gun had a clean sweep the length of the room. Dade Carleton came down behind Mike, moving with unnatural stiffness. He was very careful to keep both hands showing above the bar. When he spoke his voice was thin sounding and tight.

"Like the Sheriff says, boys; some of the men you was talkin' to in here today wasn't even around when your

64

friend was killed."

Matt Sheridan, facing toward Carleton, bent a long, cold look upwards. "No? Maybe you can explain how most of 'em named the same man as Shiloh's killer?"

"Well; Jack Arbuckle's not real popular with folks. He gets a mite cocky at times. He's got a passel of enemies who wouldn't miss him if he was dead."

Slidell leaned forward in his chair as though to arise. Mike told him to sit still and keep his hands in sight. Slidell stopped moving and looked over at the sheriff.

"This has gone far enough," Mike said quietly. "Now, when you boys get up, you keep your hands out in front of you—walk to that door—go to your horses, mount-up and light up. I'll give you one hour, then I'm coming after you with a posse and if we find you in Cow County—you'll either stay here permanently, or you'll go to jail."

Slidell remained bent over and motionless. "What you goin' to charge us with, Sheriff?"

"There's a town ordinance against carrying firearms in the city limits. We don't enforce it, but we can. That'll be a starter. It's good for six months. Another charge would be vagrancy—no visible means of support—inciting trouble—I could work up a pretty good bunch of charges. They might even get you a couple of years at the Territorial Prison."

Slidell's cloudy gaze didn't waver. "All right to stand up?" he asked.

Mike nodded. Slidell arose and the others followed his example. They went towards the door without another word, passed through and faded from sight. For a moment no one said anything, then Dade Carleton put two beer glasses on the bar and waited for Mike to notice them. The sheriff did not turn around; he crossed the room to Tom Velarde's side, and joined him in watching the progress of the four gunmen toward their horses at a hitchrail across the road. Later, when the strangers were riding north up the roadway, Mike and Tom left the saloon and watched them until they were well beyond town. Then they returned to the office where Tom put the scatter-gun back in the rack, dragged a sleeve across his forehead, and sat down upon the wall-bench.

"*Chihuahua!* They were like coiled rattlesnakes. Very deadly men, Sheriff."

"That's only half of it, Tom," Mike said from a frowning, troubled face. "I reckon I should have tended to them instead of the Skull Valleyers today—run 'em out of town before they had a chance to ask a lot of questions."

"No," Velarde murmured. "They would have found out anyway. It was their purpose. They would not have left the county until they got what they came after."

"Yeh; that's what's bothering me now. They'll go down to Skull Valley."

Velarde shrugged. His face became bland, almost serene looking. "A small thing," he said pleasantly. Mike looked across at him, and almost grinned. "You're learning fast, Tom. Yes; it's a small thing if they get to killing each other—but it won't end there now. There are too many people involved."

"Four of them; four of the Skull Valley men."

Mike got up, yawned, and wagged his head. "Nope; each of Shiloh's friends has friends; Jack Arbuckle, Locke Smith and Buel's other running-mates, have a lot of relatives in the Valley. Let one or two get killed on each side, Tom, and there'll be other strangers ride into town— heading south for the Valley—and before you know it, we'll have a first-class gun-war on our hands."

Velarde arose too. He looked thoughtful. The sheriff took off his hat, regarded the ingrained, pale dust a moment, then put it back on his head. "Get your horse and ride out of town a ways, Tom. See which way they went. If they angled around town and headed south, come down to the house and awaken me. If they kept on going north, come on back and get some rest."

"*Si*," the deputy said with a wry smile. "I am the posse you spoke of?"

Mike slapped him on the back, left the office and started homeward. At the far intersection of Grant and Front streets a shadow detached itself from the deep darkness next to a store building, and moved to intercept him. He saw it and stopped, facing around.

The face that materialised, like the voice, was softly warm. "You have a sharp eye, Mike."

"Good evening, Toni."

"I waited for you."

He looked toward the shadows. "There? Why didn't you wait at the office?"

"It's too fine a night to be cooped up, don't you think?"

"Well yes," he replied, with saddle-weariness in his legs.

"Mike; everyone in town knows about those men who rode in last night. Those friends of Shiloh Smith's."

"I expect they do. What're they saying?"

Her head was tilted back; the even, clean lines of her features were radiant in the moonlight. "They say one man will be killed if he goes up against them."

"I see. Well; I've already talked to them and they've left town. But I wasn't alone—I've got a deputy now."

"Yes, I know. I've seen him. That young Velarde boy."

"He's not as young as you'd think, Toni. He's older than you are."

"But age in a peace officer isn't measured by years, is it?"

He smiled down into her eyes. "I guess not. I guess most folks think of lawmen as craggy old goats bristling with pistols and scowls."

"Not everyone, Mike. I don't."

The same confused turmoil which had bothered him the night before, after he had kissed her, came back now, only stronger. He said roughly, "You'd better go home, Toni."

Disappointment made her wilt; it let her shoulders slump forward and her head lower a little. "All right, Mike. Good night."

"Good night."

He watched her cross the road and sway into the shadows, moving east through the quietude of Grant Street, then he continued to the home he shared with his brother, and didn't look up from a troubled contemplation of the plankwalk until he heard voices beyond the door.

When he entered, Doctor Pat and big Hugh Grant craned their heads around at him. Pat pointed towards a dish and cup on a table.

"Cold supper," he said. "Or have you eaten?"

"Nope; thanks, Pat. Hugh; what keeps you out so late?"

"You," Grant said, drawing in his bulk as the sheriff tossed his hat aside and dropped down beside him on the leather sofa. "I guess you saw the strangers."

"Yep. They just rode out of town a little while ago."

"And what did the Skull Valleyers say?"

"About what you'd expect: They don't know who killed Smith, they don't care who did it; and they aren't going to avoid trouble or stay out of town."

Grant drummed with one set of beefy fingers on a tabletop, looking straight ahead at Pat McMahon with an I-told-you-so expression on his face, and a scowl around his eyes.

"Then why don't you hire a *real* deputy, if there's going to be trouble?"

"I've got a real one, Hugh."

"Greaser . . . huh!"

"A Mex, yes, but a good one." Sheriff Mike fixed Grant with a critical look. "But I can't keep him if I can't pay him."

"Council won't go along with hiring a Mex deputy, Mike. I can tell you that right here an' now."

The sheriff continued to regard Hugh Grant for a moment, then he sighed and began to unfasten the badge on his shirt. "Here, Hugh; you better get another sheriff. This one just quit." He got up, towering large and thick. "Good night, gentlemen; it's been a long day."

Hugh Grant's voice, sharp and whiplash sounding, broke out. "Mike! Don't be silly! Here; you take back this damned badge."

Mike stood by the table looking at the cold food there. "Where'd you get the vegetables, Pat?" He asked mildly.

Grant grunted to his feet, walked heavily across the room holding the badge out. "Now listen here, Mike; you got no call to get sore over a little misunderstanding. Here; take this damned thing."

Still ignoring the blacksmith, Mike sat down at the table. The fried potatoes were black around the edges. He looked at his brother from a smooth, expressionless face. "You'll never make a cook, Pat."

Grant stumped around the chair snorting loudly. "*Here!*"

Mike looked up blandly into Grant's red face. "I guess you don't hear very good, Hugh."

Grant put the badge down beside the plate. He looked more worried than angry. "All right. Keep your Mex deputy, if you want him."

"I told him we'd pay him fifty a month and horse-care."

"All *right!*"

"But he's worth more. We'll pay him sixty a month and horse-care."

Grant's face became apoplectic. He fumed and stormed back to the couch and dropped down with an oath. Pat laughed; the sound carried beyond the house and into the still night.

"For sixty dollars a month you could get Bat Masterton, or Wyatt Earp up from Tombstone," Grant growled.

Mike pinned the badge on his shirt and said no more; while he ate Pat poured Hugh Grant a stiff drink and one for himself. He wiped his eyes before downing his. After a moment of silence Grant squirmed around on the couch to face the table. His voice was still sharp-edged with annoyance.

"Now what do we do?" he demanded of the sheriff, who continued to eat a moment before replying.

"I reckon we try to avoid a fight. If we can't do that, then

70

I guess we try to keep it down in the Valley."

"And if that doesn't work—what then?"

"Why then, the town council'd better get another sheriff—or put in a call for the army."

Grant finished his drink and regarded the glass frowningly, turning it in the fingers of one huge hand. Finally he swore with strong feeling and pushed himself upright, putting the glass aside. "Just once, I wish something'd happen in this damned country that didn't stink of trouble—just once." He picked up his hat and held it by the brim. "Tell me something, Sheriff; just how did this all start, anyway."

Mike finished eating and turned in the chair. He saw Pat's face congeal with a horrified look on it. "Shiloh Smith got bushwhacked—you know that."

"Yes, I know that; but these friends of his . . ."

"They were at Junction City waiting for him. When he didn't come up, they came looking for him."

Grant stood bear-like and glowering for a moment, then he began shaking his head. "What was Smith doing here, in the first place?"

From a corner of his eye the sheriff saw his brother making a small, frantic gesture. He ignored it and stood up. "Riding through, he told me. You know how those things happen, Hugh. Buel was troublesome sometimes. This time he choused the wrong man. It happens like that right along. Men who wear guns like to test their speed now and then. Buel had a good reputation—I guess Shiloh Smith's reputation, like his speed, was better."

"So now we got the makings of a gun-war."

"Don't worry about it, Hugh," the sheriff said affably.

"It'll blow over."

Grant looked disbelieving. He watched Mike go to the couch, sit down and begin tugging off his boots. "Good night," he said, and left the room. Not until the door slammed, hard, behind him, did Mike look across at the doctor.

"What kind of an idiot do you take me for, anyway; I wasn't going to say anything about Toni."

Pat poured a stiff drink and downed it. "I thought you might—knowing you and your peculiar principles."

"If you're not planning on drinking all that whiskey yourself, I'd admire a glass of it," Mike said, working at his shirt-front, finally casting the garment aside as Pat leaned far forward holding out a glass. "You drink too much of that stuff, Pat."

"Why don't you mind your own business."

"I do. I also mind yours, since you don't have sense enough to."

Pat looked at the glass in his hand, put it aside with a sigh and leaned back in his chair. "Just this once, let's go to bed without being mad at one another."

Mike raised the glass. "I'll drink to that." He downed the fiery liquor, made a face, and put the glass beside Hugh Grant's empty one. "Now tell me about all the babies you delivered today."

A shadow of annoyance passed over the doctor's face. "I didn't deliver any kids today—and that damned Fred Nolan didn't finish the dental chair harness, either, and I had three extractions to do."

"Why didn't he; he hasn't been too busy lately."

"He said he had a rush order to make a pistol holster for

a thirty-two. Someday, out here, people will—"

"A thirty-two calibre pistol?" Mike asked, perplexedly.

Pat shrugged. "That's what he said."

"But that's a woman's gun."

"You know I know nothing about guns, Mike. Besides; what difference does it make?"

Mike's face was thoughtful, and slightly marred by a frown when he answered. "Well now; it just depends on who the woman is he was making it for."

CHAPTER FIVE

IT WAS DARK out with a spreading hint of azure in the east when a fisted hand beat upon the front door of the McMahon house, and a voice cried: "Sheriff!" in hard-breathing excitement.

Mike awakened, sat bolt upright, and listened to the patter of slippered feet hurrying down the hall from Pat's room. The pounding became louder, quivering through the house in echoing waves, then it ceased suddenly, and Mike, pulling on trousers, boots, scooping up his shirt and gun and hastening toward the door, heard voices in the parlour.

It was Tom Velarde. His face was alive with urgency, and as Pat fought to light a lamp, he said, "Sheriff; they are in the Valley."

"Did you follow them there? Is that where you've been all night?"

"*Si.* I wanted to be sure. They went north as far as the shale beds, then eastward to Blue River, then down it southward, and finally, when they thought they were not being followed, they followed Casadora Creek to the stage-road."

"And down into the Valley," Mike finished. Lamplight brightened with gradual intentness until the room was aglow. Mike shrugged into his shirt, pushed the tails inside his trousers and spoke aside to his brother as he moved toward the hallway.

"Feed him, Pat. I'll be back directly."

He got his gun-belt and hat, rubbed a hand over the bristle along his jaw, shrugged and returned to the parlour. Pat was flapping around in a long white nightshirt, nearly as excited as the deputy was. Mike got a cup of coffee, made a cigarette to go along with it, and sat down at the table while Tomas ate. Finally he said, "Something I want you to do for me today, Pat. Find out who Nolan's making that thirty-two holster for."

"All right. Mike; hadn't you better round up a posse?"

"Don't have the time," the sheriff replied. "Anyway, it'd take hours to get anyone up at this hour." He got up. "Ready, Tom?"

"*Seguro, jefe.*"

"Then let's get you a fresh horse, and be on our way."

At the liverybarn they had to awaken the nighthawk to secure a fresh mount for Velarde, then they left Vacaville in a stiff trot, south-bound. They spoke rarely, and not until they reached the creek did Sheriff McMahon ask: "Tom; are you sure there were only four riders?"

"I am sure, Sheriff." The dark eyes, ringed now by dark shadows, regarded the larger man for a moment. "Did you expect there to be more?"

"I didn't know, Tom. I just sort of wondered if maybe Hank Hubbel wasn't with them."

"Hubbel?" The Mexican said, on a rising note. "The man who now runs the liverybarn?"

Mike nodded, swinging back into the saddle and drawing his horse away from the water. "Yeah; he's in this too."

Velarde sprang up and edged his mount over beside the sheriff. As they were jogging down into the Valley again, he said, "He may be, as you say, in this, too, *jefe,* but I doubt this very much. Yesterday, about midday, Hubbel rode out of the liverybarn with a bedroll behind his saddle. He rode west, toward Tombstone."

Mike looked around, surprised. "Hubbel? Are you sure?"

"*Si;* very sure."

Mike was silent for a long, solid moment, then he laughed. "It must've been a hard decision to make, Tom."

"*Que?* What decision, *jefe?*"

"Whether to hang around and wait for Miss Parker to fall into his arms, and maybe the liverybarn too, or hightail it before Shiloh Smith's friends found out who sent for Smith—and thereby got him killed."

"No *Señor,* not such a difficult decision. A man will gamble many times in his lifetime, but he does not do it more than a few times with his life at stake. Not a man like Hank Hubbel."

They rode steadily down the paling land. Far out the mountains were pink tinted, soft and inviting appearing; the shallow, grey earth sparkled from mica flakes in the barren soil. Gradually, as time passed all this changed. The mountains became smoky from heat-haze, the desert turned sullen, bitter looking and dusty, and by the time they heard the shooting, faint 'pops' carried for miles on the still air, the heat was rising around them, and the sun was a molten disc hanging in a faded sky.

Mike lifted his horse into a loose lope, bearing south-easterly. As Tom spurred up beside him, he called out: "The Arbuckle place," then swore a passionate oath.

They came to a dry creek bed, clattered across it, and as long as the way lay open, they rode a loose-rein, bending their horses around prickly pitahaya and graceful, spidery paloverde bushes—called trees by some, but hardly that. Then they drew up suddenly, listening. The bright sunlight danced around them bringing with it clouds of white dust, but not a sound.

"It is over," Tom said, with an undertone of tragic meaning.

"It better not be," Mike ripped out. "Come on; just a little farther."

A sloping land swell cut off their view. They topped out over it and Mike threw up a hand, reining back. The smell of smoke was strong here. Farther out, following the course of uneven land, was a fenced off clearing with trees and greenery. Yellow flames, the colour of sunlight, twisted upwards in jerky motion from an outbuilding. Velarde shaded his eyes.

"Is that the Arbuckle place?"

"Yes."

"I see no movement, *jefe.*"

Mike was silent. After a moment he reined out, moving slowly down toward the ranch. Except for the crackling of fire, the area was still and hushed. He stopped and called out: "Hello—the house!" Echoes chased themselves into the distance and faded. He called again, then, receiving no answer, pushed forward until the heat stung his eyes. As he dismounted, studying the house, seeing the broken windows, the evidence of a long battle, he spoke from the corner of his mouth.

"Ride out a ways, Tom. See if you can pick up the trail of the attackers. Watch out for an ambush."

After Velarde had trotted away, easterly, Mike looped his reins and went up to the front of the house. The door was hanging open. He was about to push inside when he heard Tom's voice, a high, keening call which was wordless; he turned. The deputy was bending from the saddle looking down.

"*Jefe!* Here—this is Jack Arbuckle."

Mike waved understanding, gazed briefly at the dark sprawl mid-way between house and barn, then turned back toward the door. A rifle barrel was there, pointing upwards towards his face. In the gloom beyond he could not make out its holder.

"It's the sheriff," he called softly. "Point that thing away."

When the gun drooped, he entered the house. Two women, one no more than forty but looking much older, the other young and, in a plain way, attractive, watched him turn around looking at the wreckage. An old man was sitting in a chair staring straight ahead. Mike approached him, then saw that he was held upright by a propped gun, and although his eyes were open he was dead. The older woman spoke, dull-voiced and croaking.

"'Come along a while after midnight and commenced shootin.' We was abed. Jackie tried to get a horse to go for help." She let the gun in her hands fall away. She drew herself upright with an effort. "He's a-lyin' out there. They kep' shootin' into him long after he was dead."

Mike looked at the girl. "Make some coffee," he said, then drew up a chair for the woman as the girl moved unseeingly and dutifully from the parlour.

"Paw thought they was Injuns—at first. We'd a stood 'em off, Sheriff—but they got paw when he tried to talk to 'em. Warn't Injuns—they was whites."

"What did they say to you?"

"That they wanted Jackie."

"And after he was killed . . . ?"

"They jes' lay out there shootin', makin' sport of it. Shootin' into Jackie—then into the house. Then they quit." The anguished eyes went to Mike's face. "They said Jackie shot their frien' in Vacaville—tain't so, Sheriff. He never done it."

"I know, Mrs. Arbuckle." Mike straightened up as Tom came through the door, staring around him; staring longest at the propped-up dead man in the chair.

"Find anything?" Mike asked.

"Tracks, yes. Four men—but we knew this. And these," Velarde held out a handful of cartridge cases.

Mike took them, studied them briefly and closed his fist around them. "No bodies?"

"None."

"That's too bad."

The girl re-entered the room with coffee. The older woman drank it mechanically and Mike gave his cup to the deputy.

Suddenly the woman spoke, without looking up, in fact without being actually aware of their presence. "It was Locke killed their friend—not Jackie."

"Are you sure, Miz' Arbuckle?" Mike asked.

A nod, slow and burdened. "Jackie told us just before he tried to get to the horses. Said we ought to know in case somethin' happened to him. 'Said it was Locke Hibbard."

Mike looked inquiringly at the girl. She nodded, looking into his face, but she did not speak. Tom Velarde put his cup down very quietly and watched the sheriff, who turned toward the door. From just over the threshold he spoke softly to the girl.

"Take care of her; we'll send help."

The fire was dwindling, having consumed the out-building; its heat radiated outward in waves, nor did Mike and Tom escape it until they were a quarter mile away, fol-lowing the trail of the four horsemen. At a sump-well where they stopped to drink and water the horses, Mike followed the direction of the killers with his eyes, and he was puzzled. The gunmen were not riding toward Mexico, as he had fully expected; they were making toward the mountains far north of Vacaville, which meant they would be visible for miles across the desert, or at least their dust-banner would be visible.

"They've got a destination in mind," he told the deputy. "Maybe they know this country better than I thought. I'm sure I never saw any of them around here before, though."

"Many men travel this way, *jefe,* in the night—from Mexico. They would come to know their way."

"But why north, Tom? Mexico is south. They would be safe there. No matter where they go, north, the law'll be after them."

"Those men have no fear of the law, Sheriff. They are outlaws, killers, bad men—they laugh at the law."

"Uh huh," Mike muttered. "Well; they better have a real

good laugh. Come on; we'll go as far as the Stone Gorman place. Maybe the old man'll give us fresh horses."

"*Señor* Gorman is not a friendly man. I don't know . . ."

Mike picked his way easterly, saying, "There aren't very many friendly men anywhere in Skull Valley, Tom, but when something like that massacre back there wipes out their neighbours, I think they'll be at least co-operative."

Nor was the sheriff wrong. Stone Gorman, a gaunt recluse of a man, big and rangy and mean looking, listened with a savage expression as Mike told him what had happened at the Arbuckle ranch, then, without speaking, he flagged an arm toward the corral and headed toward the house. When he emerged moments later, as Mike and Tom were mounting fresh horses, he had a gun about his waist and a carbine in one grimy fist. "Wait," he ordered, "till I saddle up."

"No need for that," the sheriff said. "You ride over to Pratly's, and round up some folks to go over to Arbuckle's and take care of things."

Gorman stopped as he went through the corral gate and looked flintily at Mike. "What fer? They're dead ain't they?"

"Mrs. Arbuckle and the girl aren't."

"Women!" Gorman said fiercely. " 'Got no business in this country anyway." After he disappeared into the barn, Mike winked at Tom and they set their horses into a long lope. They were disappearing beyond the farthest paloverde bush when Stone Gorman's head popped out of the barn door. He watched them fade from sight for a moment, then thickened the clear air with lurid curses and went back into the barn. When he emerged later, astride a big, ugly-headed bay horse, he set his course toward the Arbuckle place, riding with flapping arms, a big, gaunt scarecrow of a man in soiled clothing and a nearly brimless hat.

They trailed the gunmen in a large-spending curve which took them out and around Vacaville, and for a while Mike thought they might be heading for Junction City. Then it became apparent that their route was northward toward the far-out mountains.

By mid-afternoon their stock was wearying and they, themselves, particularly Tomas who had had no rest the night before, were wilting from the curling heat. Finally, sighting a ranch house in the near distance they made for it, and there, a lone man, as dirty and grimy as the sheriff and his deputy were, welcomed them with a gourd full of spring-water. The man said little, and when they asked for fresh horses he spread his hands deploringly.

"On'y got one horse—my own saddle animal—an' I need him."

They pushed on, with the heat moving against them, until Sheriff Mike saw that Tom could not go much farther. He halted in the blistering shade of a sandstone boulder, made a cigarette and said, "Tom; you go back to town. Hunt up my brother and Hugh Grant and tell them to make up a posse and trail me. . . . And Tom; you stay in town; get some rest."

"*Seguro, jefe,*" the Mexican replied. "I will get the posse."

Mike looked out steadily from slitted eyes. "And stay in town."

"But, Sheriff; I am a good tracker. And—"

"Yes, I know: And you aren't tired. Well; the point is—if those Skull Valley people decide to come to Vacaville hunting for someone to get mad at, I'd like to know there's a good law officer there to stop them."

Velarde's sunken, reddened eyes brightened a little. *"Comprendo, Señor; pardona mi.* I will watch the town."

Mike smoked, standing beside his resting mount, watching little puffs of dust spurt upwards from the hooves of his deputy's mount. He smiled through cracked lips, ground out the cigarette, mounted, and sat for a moment looking far out where the bony flanks of the Galiuros squatted low upon the plain. There were not many ranches or settlers in the arid land ahead. He could tick them off in his mind, and, with the exception of one or two newcomers he'd heard about, homesteaders, but had never met, he knew them all.

Riding northward again, but slowly now because he was alone, the heat lessened on his right side and burned more directly on his left side. It was a long two hours before he saw a shack ahead. Beside it, enclosed in a faggot-corral, were three drowsing horses. On the far side of the shack, also enclosed by a faggot-fence, was a sparse and wilting garden of vegetables. His interest arose; this was clearly one of the newcomers to Cow County. There were not many; in fact they were so few, and usually so poor, that as yet the cowmen recognised in them no threat to the unfenced ranges.

Mike swung westerly from the outlaws' trail and plodded up to the house. He tied his horse in the only shade and started forward. A sharp-shouldered man, thin as a rail, was watching him from the slab-roofed front porch. He had a rifle in his hand but no belt-gun, and his lean, blistered face, as red as a lobster, had an unwelcome set to it. When the sheriff said "Howdy," and moved into the shade, the homesteader nodded once and grunted.

"Seen any riders go by lately?" Mike asked, studying the man carefully.

"No."

"Well; maybe you heard 'em. They went by about an hour ago—not much more'n that."

"Ain't seen nor heard nothing, Marshal."

"Just sheriff will do," Mike said with a slow smile. "Sheriff McMahon. I guess I haven't been out this way since you folks settled here. Mind if I ask your name?"

"Ed Ward."

"Well; glad to have you in Cow County, Mister Ward."

"Ain't glad to be here," the homesteader said bitterly.

Mike looked toward the corral. "Your horses?"

"Yes. Two're team critters, the sorrel's my saddle critter."

"Could I borrow one of them? The horse I'm riding is leg-weary and hungry. Got him down in Skull Valley."

"Skull Valley? You rid that fur today?"

"Yes."

Ward began shaking his head; he kept on doing it while he spoke. "Nope; man'd ride a critter that hard wouldn't do my old saddlehorse any good. What's the hurry?"

"Four riders passed this way—not more than a quarter mile out, in fact—attacked a ranch down there last night and killed two men."

"Fair fight?" Ward asked, dour glance on Mike's face. The answer he got was dry and quiet.

"No; I wouldn't be chasing them if it had been. Well; I'll

be pushing on."

Mike went to his horse, untied and swung up, rode along the side of the faggot corral gazing in, then boosted his mount into a slow lope and rocketed along for half a mile before he found the killers' trail again. Then he slowed to a walk and held to it as far as the first lift of canyons. By then the sun was sliding rapidly toward the west, and down where he was, the world was cooling; sending up acrid odours from creosote bush, sage, and hot granite. He pushed on as far as a seepage spring, easterly, and there off-saddled, hobbled his horse and turned it loose to drink, roll, and graze.

Southwesterly lay Vacaville. He could faintly make it out hard down the horizon. If he hadn't been on high ground it would have been invisible. As it was, there was only a dark blur, shifting in the fading light. He made a cigarette, smoked it with his hat off and sweat drying pleasantly on his body. He ached and hunger gnawed inside, but these things were not uppermost in his mind. For a while he blocked in squares of desert until he found the squatter's shack. His gaze rested there a long time before it moved off, trailed up along the shading thrust of mountains. Somewhere up there, were his killers. Night would catch them, too. He doubted if they knew the land they were in as well as he did, and from that he drew comfort. There were few waterholes in the Galiuros.

Looseness settled over him, spreading out along his frame, and except for hunger he was content to sit there, back against a hard push of stone, drawn-out shadows around him. Higher, up along the ragged peaks where the sun still shone, there lay a soft saffron light. While he watched, it changed subtly, turning to a greeny purple. Then it faded out into coral pink, and this darkened slowly to red as the sun fell lower, until the hot and barren pinnacles were the colour of blood, then, with its customary swiftness, the sun was gone and only a fading glow remained aloft.

Darkness would not fall full down until nine o'clock. If the posse moved swiftly it could find him before then.

He lay back and slept, and although soft pain and weariness were deep in him, his granite bed did not permit too deep a slumber. Later, when the clatter of horsemen approaching over gravelly ground came discordantly through the near-dark, he heard it and got up. It came from the direction of Vacaville, but he waited until recognisable voices were distinguishable before he called out.

The first man to dismount was cursing, puffing, Hugh Grant. The second man was Doctor Pat. Farther back, picking his way up the canyon, was the saddlemaker, Fred Nolan. Beside him, Charley Householder's nightbarman, Will Herman. They were the last up, and the last to dismount. Both got down as Hugh Grant had, with groaning profanity. Mike took a small packet from his brother and smelt bread and onions. "Thanks, Pat. I guess Tom told you what we found."

Hugh Grant sat down gingerly. "Yes; he told us. Where are the varmints?"

"Somewhere back there in the hills," Mike replied, chewing the sandwich Pat had brought for him. "I think we can get them tonight."

Grant, probing the inside of one large leg gingerly, looked up. "Tonight?" he said explosively.

Mike grinned. "Sure; I know this country pretty well. We'll leave the horses here and hunt 'em afoot. They won't be far away."

Grant's head raised slowly, higher and higher, up along the thinly visible peaks. "Well," he said at last, "I'll stay here and mind the horses."

Will Herman snickered. When Grant's stony scowl found his face, the noise died abruptly. Nolan came forward and eased down upon the ground, near where Doctor Pat was standing, gazing outward over the ghostly plain.

"There's a squatter south of here a little ways," he said, "Name of Ward."

Mike nodded. "Yeah; I know. Hugh; why don't you ride down to Ward's shack and take him back to town with you?"

Three sets of eyes went to Mike's face in swift movement. Grant stopped rubbing his leg. "Ward? You mean that stone-rancher back there, where we passed by?"

Mike nodded and Doctor Pat said: "Why? He's not one of them, is he?"

"No; I didn't recognise him as one of them; but he helped at least one man by giving him a fresh horse. That sorrel saddle animal in his corral's been ridden into the ground."

"He could have done that himself," Will Herman said. "He's got a few cows, too."

Mike shook his head. "I asked him if he'd seen or heard riders pass by. He said he hadn't. Well; the tracks went within a quarter mile of the house, and even if one set hadn't turned in back there, Ward would have noticed four men riding by." Mike got up stiffly, and stretched. "I know how it is, with these squatters—they're hungry. They'll do just about anything for a few dollars. But trying to mislead the law's pretty serious, too. Particularly now." The grey-level eyes stayed on Hugh Grant's face. "How about it, Hugh?"

The fat man pushed himself upright. He was still frowning. "Well; all right, Mike. But I'd feel less like a shirker if I stayed here—at least with the horses."

"The horses will be all right. We'll leave them tied."

Grant sprung his legs a little, tentatively, and grimaced. "Shoe 'em yes," he said "Ride 'em, no." As he waddled toward the horses he added: "All right; I'll take Ward in and turn him over to your deputy. 'Want me to send back more men?"

Mike said, "No," and looked down at Nolan. "Say Fred; something I'm curious about. Who'd you make a thirty-two holster for?"

"Toni Parker; why?"

"No particular reason," the sheriff answered. "I just wondered." He went to his saddle, got his carbine, and straightened up. "Come on; we'll try to make as much time as possible before the moon comes up."

They left the horses, following Mike. Over his shoulder the sheriff said: "Stay close and don't make any noise." This was the darkest time of the night, before moonrise and several hours after sunset. It was a time that blinded men with gloom and dense shadows, and of course it was inevitable that they should stumble against unseen boulders, curse to themselves and struggle on. Of the four, the McMahon brothers were most adept. Will Herman, a townsman by choice, was as much out of his element as was Nolan the saddlemaker. The difference between

Herman and Nolan was basically one of character. Herman tried to be silent, watchful, Nolan did not. It was his way to forge ahead, to disdain the superior knowledge of others; to seek to lead, in an element where he was clearly out of place. Twice Sheriff Mike had to tell him to stay back.

The dark hush of night was thick. Heavy currents of rising air, acid-smelling and hot, came down the canyons to wash against them. The sheriff, who had hunted both rene-gade Indians and rustlers in the Galiuros, knew his way. A mile or more to his right was a red-stone ledge. Below it a spring came out of the rocks and ran down the canyon for a mile, leaving visible greenery. Knowing the wanted men had struck into the mountains before sunset, and realising their need for water, and realising they would be looking for it, he concluded they would be encamped somewhere near the little spring.

As he led the others anglingly across the base of the mountains, the sky brightened; became pewter coloured and soft appearing. The stars were dimly visible. He swung a long glance along the horizon until he saw the pale glow where the moon would rise. Finally, he stopped in a jumble of boulders awaiting the others. Then he raised his arm, pointing ahead.

"See that ledge? Below it's a spring. I think, if they saw the cottonwoods and green grass, they'll have camped there."

Will Herman puffed out his cheeks and let go a long sigh. "I hope so," he said fervently. "My shins're blue from crashing into boulders."

Nolan made a cigarette, cupped his hands around the match and blew out a streamer of smoke. "What're they doing up in here, anyway?" he asked Mike.

The sheriff shrugged without replying. Doctor Pat was examining a torn sleeve. He looked around at the saddle-maker. "Going north, obviously."

"Mexico's south," the saddlemaker said, flatly.

Mike, who had been seeking the pinpoint of a cooking-fire, which he never found, straightened up. "You're dead right," he said to Nolan. "Mexico would have been the best place for them, right now."

Will Herman, looking up from his examination of a lac-erated leg, said, "They can still make it, too. They've got horses and we're afoot."

The sheriff watched Nolan snuff out his cigarette and replied. "If we make enough noise they'll hear us and get away for sure. Unless we did all this climbing for nothing we'll have to be still as Indians from here on." He jerked his head at Herman. "Come on; that moon isn't going to help us any."

They went forward again; rested, bruised, but with extreme caution. Even Nolan stayed in his place, head swinging from side to side, eyes working into the shadows around them.

Mike stopped again, a half hour later, testing the air. When Pat crept up beside him, the sheriff said, "Smoke." He motioned for them all to get down and crawl. By set-ting an example, he led them another hundred yards. Then the moon soared over the rim of the desert and silver light flooded outward.

Mike's crawl slowed gradually, until it stopped alto-gether. When the others came up beside him and lay belly-down on the warm lip of land which fell away sharply below them, the sheriff thrust his arm out, pointing up the canyon a short ways, and he whispered: "There."

Triumph was in the word.

CHAPTER SIX

A GLADE, not more than an acre in size, lay beneath the red-stone ledge. Green grass was rank there, and moving darkly against the backdrop of ghost-lighted mountain, were four hobbled horses. Nearer, with a faint showing of smoke eddying around it, was a man-high rock, evidently tumbled from the heights in ages gone. A man appeared around it, on the right side. He was smoking. In his right hand was a tin cup. He stood still, looking out and around for a moment, then he disappeared behind the boulder and his words came distinctly down the night to Sheriff Mike.

"Probably a coyote. That damned horse is always stickin' his head in the air anyway."

For a while there was only a tired mutter of voices, then the same man spoke again.

". . . We paid 'em back," the voice said swiftly. "Anyway, if Shiloh'd waited for us to go along, too, it wouldn't have happened. Not like that, anyway."

A garrulous tone arose, weary sounding and grumpy. "Bushwhackers most often get their man. If we'd been there maybe this one'd gotten someone else, too."

Then the soft, slurring voice of the Mexican came softly into the night. "*Si;* it is true. But he wouldn't have gotten away—this assassin—and we wouldn't have had to kill our horses like this, leaving Cow County."

"Oh hell; go to sleep."

"No," the Mexican said, "I think one of us must watch."

"Watch?" A voice said irritably. "Why; that sheriff'll be down there buryin' Arbuckle. He couldn't trail us in the night with an Apache to smell tracks for him."

"*If* he stayed down there—but he looked to me like a man who does not waste time, *amigo.* I don't want to be caught sleeping."

"All right; you sit up then."

Mike was raising up when another voice said, "Say, Curt; what's on the other side of these mountains?"

Slidell's voice, hard and sharp, replied: "More damned mountains—then the trace. Three, four more days headin' northwest and we'll hit Idaho. Then Cow County can go suck eggs—they can't get us back."

The same questioning voice rose again. "Are you sure about that bank at Mormon Ferry?"

" 'You think I'd be ridin' in this direction if I wasn't sure of it? They got over thirty thousand dollars in that cow-town bank. If I didn't know this for a fact, believe me, we'd be deep in Mexico by this time—'stead of ridin' our rears raw getting away from that smart-alec sheriff."

The Mexican spoke softly, and his words barely carried to the motionless men on the lip of land south of the outlaw encampment. "After we get *that, amigos,* we can return to Mexico and be kings." He was silent briefly, then, when he spoke again, the position of his voice had changed. "I will watch, *compadres.*"

He appeared around the side of the boulder and Mike watched him lean there, wide-shouldered, deep chested, with lean flanks and saddle warped legs. He made a cigarette, lit it making no effort to conceal the match's flare, then he pushed back his hat and settled into a position of languid watchfulness. Obviously Dominguez Belasco was more cautious than suspicious.

Mike drew the others close to him and whispered: "I'll creep down there and get him—if I'm lucky—but if he discovers me, you boys be ready. Pat; crawl north until you're behind that doggoned boulder. Nolan; you watch the down-trail from here. Will; you come with me. I'll leave you behind where you can cover both ways out of the canyon—back up the mountain, and down the creek." Mike looked into each face. "And boys," he said slowly, very distinctly, "Don't make a sound. Crawl on your hands and knees if you have to, but be quiet."

They separated, Mike and Will Herman crawling slowly over the stony earth behind a covert of mesquite and prickly chapparal. But this was the heart of the night and it was inevitable that movement should cause sound, and that sound should carry through the total silence. The air was dry, thin, and receptive; it caught and carried every rustle, every whisper, magnifying each over and over again.

As Mike crawled, followed by Will Herman, the canyon opened up ahead of them and from its unseen source the little spring sent a soft current of cool air against them. Herman, twenty feet back, saw Mike's shoulders rise and weave as he made his way through the underbrush, and once, when the sheriff paused, the bartender crawled up until he felt Mike's foot ahead of him.

On their right was the boulder. Profiled against it, jutting flatly outwards, was Dominquez Belasco. He had killed the cigarette, and stood now, head drowsing low, both arms crossed over his chest. He looked asleep but Mike was not deceived. That was the stance of a listening man.

He did not move until Belasco raised his head, looking westward, then swung it slowly to the right, taking in all the moonlighted area around them. Finally, Belasco shifted his feet, making a rustling sound in the shale, and his big-rowelled spurs tinkled softly, and he grew motionless again.

Mike continued to crawl forward as far as a stunted juniper, its trunk scarred by bear-claws. There, he put his lips to Will Herman's ear and said: "Stay here and watch him," meaning the Mexican. "If he sees me don't wait— shoot."

Herman inclined his head, eyes shifting to the still silhouette in front of the rock.

Mike had the hardest part of his journey ahead of him. Where the brush sloped downwards was loose stone and powdery earth. It would have been a miracle if he could have gotten up close to Belasco without being discovered; as it was he had crawled downward no more than a hundred feet when a shifting, soft roll of flake-rock moved under him, sending a tiny avalanche down through the sage. The sentinel's head whipped around. His arms fell to his sides and his dark-shadowed face showed tense in the moonlight.

Mike held his breath, watching through the spiney sage branches. An interminable time went by, then Belasco's body loosened although he did not look away.

With a rough curse on his lips, Mike reached forward to push back the limbs gently and squeeze onward. He advanced another fifteen feet, and could see the Mexican's face plainly, then he stopped, loosened the pistol in its holster, and remained motionless trying to estimate the time he had been crawling, in order to satisfy himself that Pat would be in place. In studying the rank greenery less than twenty feet away, Mike knew he could not get much closer before Belasco saw him. He went forward again, an inch at a time, Apache-style, then the last fringe of brush was hiding him and he had gone as far as he could go.

Groping for a stone, Mike found two lying together. Gathering his legs under him for the spring, he tossed the rocks over the sentinel's head into the undergrowth by the creek. When Belasco's head swung around, Mike stood up and lunged forward. The Mexican heard him coming. He was dropping into a crouch and whirling back when Mike's gun, swinging overhand, came down upon his head. The hat cushioned the blow but Belasco sank down into the grass without a sound.

Mike's heart was sloshing and his open mouth sucked in thin mountain air as though he could not get enough of it. He twisted from the waist, seeking Will Herman. The barman was screened by brush, and although he must have seen Mike's triumph, he did not move. Then, down at the lip of land where Nolan was watching, a carbine blew the night apart and re-echoed from the mountain walls.

Mike dropped flat in the grass, rolling to see what Nolan had fired at. Nothing was moving, but from behind the boulder there was the quick stamp of feet; the frightened trilling of sleep-thickened voices. Another gun exploded, but this was from the north, behind the boulder, and the sheriff heard his brother's voice raised in a long call.

"Throw 'em down!"

Two revolver shots slammed upwards, toward the sound of the doctor's voice. Mike heard the gunmen behind the boulder swear in grinding tones, then he got to his feet, removed Belasco's pistol from its holster and threw it backwards into the brush. He flattened against stone, drawing himself upright slowly. Less than ten feet away but protected by rock, a man's voice said: "How many are there?"

Another voice, recognisable as belonging to Curt Slidell, said, "At least two—one down the draw, another one back up behind us."

"Then let's get round to the other side of the damned boulder."

Spurs rang out and the soft fall of boots against shale brought Mike facing to his right. He saw no one, but he fired, and instantly the footfalls ceased. Into the echo of his shot a man's voice said: "Three—there's another one around front."

"Come back here, dammit. Get down."

Mike waited until a swift exchange of shots between Pat and the wanted men ended, then he called out: "Throw them down, boys; you're boxed-in."

"Go t'hell. Who is it, anyway?"

"The sheriff. Throw 'em down and walk out here or you're going back tied crossways to your saddles."

Suddenly there was silence, brooding and drawn out. Mike began a slow withdrawal into the shadows towards the creek. Only by doing that could he watch both sides of the boulder. And what he had anticipated, happened; two vague shadows, each advancing around the rock from opposite directions, came fluidly forward. He had a clear shot at the man on his left. When he fired the shadow sank against the earth; there was one, long breath, rattling harsh, then stillness again. The second shadow, farther along the rock, faded from sight.

Now Will Herman fired. A high, prolonged cry rang out, and when it diminished the savage curses of Curt Slidell could be heard.

"All right. You can quit now, Sheriff. We're whipped."

"Walk around to the south side of the rock," Mike called back. "And come unarmed."

"We're coming. Hold up, now."

Two shadows emerged, one arrow-straight and balancing on the balls of its feet, the other shadow bent over and moving with difficulty. When the moon struck down near where Belasco lay, Mike could see their faces; it was Curt Slidell and Matthew Sheridan, the latter evidently wounded from Will Herman's shot.

"Pat," the sheriff called out, "Come down behind them. Will—cover them." He walked out into the pewter light, went as far as Sheridan, and reached forward to pull the man erect. There was a black streamer of blood on the injured man's right side. He stood erect with gasping effort.

"Pat; hurry up."

When the doctor came down through the crackling brush and across the little glade, Curt Slidell twisted to watch his approach.

"Will; get Fred and come on down here," Mike called. Later, when they were standing together, the sheriff sent Nolan after their horses, and detailed Herman to saddle the outlaws' animals.

Doctor Pat lay aside his carbine and squinted at

Sheridan's wound. He shook his head. "Bleeding pretty bad, Mike. If we can stop that he'll make it all right. Looks like three broken ribs." Placing both hands on the injured man, Pat forced him to lie down in the grass, where he could improvise a bandage better. As he worked, Mike pointed with his pistol toward Belasco.

"Help him up," he ordered Slidell.

"Ought to split his skull," the outlaw said, but bent, grasped the Mexican's shirt, and lifted. Belasco's knees were like rubber. He moaned and staggered while Slidell's arm steadied him. Then he felt his head and looked around stupidly.

"*Que paso?*"

"You went to sleep," Slidell said fiercely.

Mike shook his head. "No he didn't; I put him to sleep."

"Same thing," Slidell growled, not looking at Mike.

"Where is Lowndes?" The Mexican asked, pinching his eyes nearly closed and peering around.

"Dead," Slidell said in the same tone. "Dead over there by that rock."

The Mexican turned and stared. "Dead?" he said dazedly.

Before Slidell could reply, Sheriff Mike tilted his gun toward him. "I told you yesterday Jack Arbuckle wasn't the man you wanted. Now I've got proof he didn't kill Smith."

Slidell looked around. He held his head low and peered upwards out of an evil and whisker-stubbled face. "Little late, ain't it?"

"For you, yes."

"How'd you find us."

"Like Belasco here, told you—I followed your tracks before daylight ended." Mike replied. "And Slidell—I'm sure sorry you won't be able to rob that bank at Mormon Ferry, over in Idaho."

The outlaw's eyes widened. "How long you lie out there listenin'?"

Mike did not answer. Will Herman came up leading the four saddled horses. He made Slidell and Belasco tie Doughbelly Lowndes across his saddle. When they finished he searched them both for hide-out guns, then ordered them to mount up. While Will held their horses, Sheriff Mike tied one leg of each man to the stirrup, lashed their hands behind them, and helped Doctor Pat get Matt Sheridan onto a horse. The wounded killer's face was the colour of slate. He sat hunched far over and the play of moonlight across his face showed where muscles rippled as he ground his teeth in pain.

When Nolan returned with the horses, Mike's posse started back. They made slow progress as far as the homesteader's shack. There, they halted for fresh bandaging material and a fast-fading woman in her early thirties turned on the sheriff like a panther.

"You!" She lashed out. "A sheriff! Why; you're no more than a—a—bully!"

Doctor Pat nodded sympathetically, and in the smoky light of a lantern no one could see the humour in his eyes. "He is that, madam; a bully. Now; will you give me some clean cloth for this man?"

When Mrs. Ward swung away, entered the shack with pounding feet, Sheriff Mike looked long at his brother. "Thanks," he said. The doctor was busy with his patient. He looked up very briefly.

"Don't mention it," he said.

When the woman returned she knelt brusquely, elbowing Pat aside, and her deft, quick fingers staunched the flow of blood and made an efficient bandage. She worked in total silence, a grim and bitter expression around her mouth. Pat watched, first with annoyance, then with interest, and finally, when Sheridan sat up, gazing at his benefactoress. Doctor Pat touched her arm as she stood up.

"Tell me, Mrs. Ward—where did you learn to bandage like that?"

"In the East—now take that—"

"Please," the doctor interrupted. "You weren't by any chance a trained nurse, were you?"

"I was—not that it's any of your business—coming out here and arresting my husband when all he did was sell a horse to keep us from—"

"Lady," Mike said shortly. "That's not all your husband did. He lied to me; and if those men had been here when he did that, I might be dead this minute."

Eliza Ward's hot stare wavered before the sheriff's steady regard. She moved away, towards the cabin door. "All right; it was wrong—but Ed had no choice—it was money . . ."

Mike jerked his head and Will Herman helped Sheridan off the porch toward the horses. Mike moved to follow Herman when Doctor Pat said: "Mrs. Ward—where were you a nurse?"

"In Indiana—and during the war—what difference does it make?"

Pat was smiling down at the thin, un-pretty face. "Because I'm a doctor, ma'm, and you're the first real nurse I've seen in this godforsaken land—and I need you."

Eliza Ward looked up at Pat perplexedly. "Are you ill, too?"

"No; I said I was a doctor—a medical doctor. I need a nurse in my office at Vacaville. I'll pay you well. Please come back to town with us."

"Now?" Eliza Ward said with a blank look.

"Yes; I'll saddle the sorrel horse in the corral for you."

"No; that's a team critter—he's not broke to ride."

"Then I'll hitch up your wagon and you can drive along with us."

Mrs. Ward's glance went past Pat to where Will Herman and Nolan were struggling to hoist the weakly cursing body of Matthew Sheridan into the saddle. "Wait," she called sharply. "Put him down." To Pat she said: "All right; the harness is in the shed, the wagon's 'round back—and when you bring it, have your friends put the injured one in the wagon on some straw."

Pat murmured "Yes'm," and moved off the porch. As he passed Mike and saw the sheriff looking at him, he raised and lowered his shoulders. "That's how you tell they're good nurses—they're bossy."

The cavalcade made its way down the ghostly land to the accompaniment of steel tyres grinding into the desert's dust and shale. Fred Nolan edged up beside Curt Slidell and craned his neck. Slidell turned and shot him a baleful glare.

"What'n hell you starin' at, you scrawny little weasel?"

"You. You're the first genuine outlaw I've ever seen captured."

Slidell turned away. On the far side of him Dominguez Belasco's teeth glistened in a strong smile. To Nolan he said: "*Amigo;* You must have a good look. If either of us get free—we, too, will remember."

Nolan straightened in the saddle, and when Mike growled at him, he dropped back to ride beside the drowsing bartender. Mike let Slidell's mount come up beside him.

"You picked a bad county to get caught in, Slidell."

"Yeh; it's bad all right—plain putrid."

"I didn't mean that way—I meant that the people of Skull Valley are a vengeful lot."

"To hell with them." Slidell thought a moment, then looked Mike squarely in the face. "I'm a sort of vengeful feller myself, mister law. You'll see what I mean when I'm loose."

"Not when, Slidell—if. We have a pretty stony old circuit judge. He's long on rope and short on patience with murderers."

"*Señor*," Belasco said. "We murdered no one. It was a fair fight. We called to Arbuckle to come out—he fired on us . . ." The Mexican rolled his head to one side. "We killed him—but in a fair fight."

"You tell the judge that," Mike said. "There were women in that house—another thing—you killed Jack Arbuckle's father. He wasn't guilty of anything, either."

"But he fired on us, *Señor.*"

Mike looked impatient. "In defence of his home, *hombre,* which is his legal right. Hold it. Keep the rest of it for your trial. I'm not the judge—just the arresting officer."

Belasco's words died on his lips as Mike urged his mount ahead, where Pat was riding beside the Ward wagon. When he came up his brother looked around. Eliza Ward glanced at him once, then looked straight ahead. Mike took off his hat, scratched his head and replaced the hat. "Mrs. Ward," he said evenly, "I didn't want to arrest your husband. I just didn't want him behind me when I was going into the hills after these men."

"Humph! Ed was no threat to you. He can't hit the broad side of a barn from the inside, with a gun."

"All right; I'll release him when we get to town."

Eliza Ward was unrelenting. She did not speak for a long time. Finally Pat said: "What did your husband do in the East, ma'm?"

"He was a liveryman—one of the best, too. Ed's forgotten more about horses and rigs than anyone in this hell-hole ever knew."

The doctor struck the pommel of his saddle with his palm and looked across at the sheriff in triumph. "See," he crowed. "A replacement for Reed Benton."

"For Hank Hubbel you mean." Mike gazed at the woman. "Did your husband ever manage a barn?"

"Certainly he managed them. Some of the best in Indiana."

"In that case I think we've got a spot for him in Vacaville. The town liverybarn's fresh out of managers."

Eliza Ward unbent briefly and looked at Mike. She did not speak until her face was averted, still held high and rock-hard. "In town?"

"Yes'm."

"Around other people—with stores and—and . . ." Her grim mouth shook but iron control came up speedily and she said no more; drove along looking straight across the desert, profile uncompromisingly stern, and lost to sight of the men on either side of the wagon, a mistiness obscured her vision.

They stopped once, when they came to the north-south stage road, and checked the ropes on Belasco. The man in the wagon was asking for water. Doctor Pat gave him a long pull at his canteen. He then asked for a smoke and Mike made him a cigarette, lit it, and stuck it in his mouth. Sheridan regarded the sheriff over the red tip of the brown-paper smoke.

"Are you the one that shot me, Sheriff?"

Mike shook his head without replying to the question. "How do you feel?"

"Like a gut-shot steer. How'm I supposed to feel?"

"Like a gut-shot steer. Sheridan; who shot Jack Arbuckle?"

The wounded man nodded toward the led-horse behind Will Herman. "It won't make no difference about you knowing. Lowndes did it. When the kid run out'n the house Doughbelly said 'he's mine,' and the rest of us waited to see if he could hit him. The kid was running hard." Sheridan's gaze went to the stiffening corpse tied across the saddle. "Doughbelly was a crack shot. When he let 'er fly the kid hit the dirt and skidded five feet."

"Then you all fired into him."

"Yeah—after some woman in the house let out a scream."

Mike looked from Slidell to Belasco, then went to his horse, swung up, and motioned for the others to start out. He remained to one side of the stage road until Will Herman came by, then he fell in with him. "Did you hear that, Will?"

"I heard it. Hanging's too good for them, Mike."

"Yeah. I'd even feel better if it'd been the real killer."

Herman's face was grey in the moonlight. "Who really did kill Shiloh Smith?"

Mike began making a cigarette. When he was finished he held the sack out. "Smoke?"

"No thanks; don't use it. Who did kill Smith, Sheriff?"

"What's the difference?"

"Folks in town'd like to know."

Mike looked at the barman. "Listen, Will," he said. "When we get back to town you just forget all this—at least don't go stirring up trouble over the bar."

"You know me better'n that, Sheriff."

"Maybe. I hope so, Will, because I'll have to keep these whelps locked up for a week or more, until the judge gets back, and I'd hate to have a lynch-mob start a ruckus on the strength of what you told 'em."

Will Herman's brows drew down in a scowl. He faced forward and watched the dim and sparse lights of Vacaville come toward them. He did not speak again until they were on the outskirts of town, then he said, "Sheriff; nothing I could say is going to make those Skull Valleyers feel kindly toward the law for bringing these men in alive."

Mike had no idea how completely true Herman's words were until they were near enough to see lanterns waving and hear the loud cry of voices. He stopped the posse with an upflung arm; sat there looking down the night at the shifting, flowing crowd of people a moment, then turned as Doctor Pat reined up.

"Looks like a lynch-mob," he said conversationally. "Must be pretty worked up, to stay up this late for a peek at the prisoners."

"From the sound," his brother said dryly, "I think they want more than just a peek." Pat swung around to look at the sheriff. "Those are pretty big odds, Mike."

"Sure are."

"Aren't you a little worried? You don't want Slidell and the Mexican lynched do you?"

Mike continued his straight-ahead stare. "No," he said finally, slowly. "I'm like Hugh Grant: I don't believe in lynch-law." The sheriff straightened up in the saddle, dug into a pocket and produced a key. "Here, Pat; that unlocks the back door of the jailhouse. You and Nolan take Slidell and Belasco out around town and come into the back alley from the south. Stay in the alley, Pat, and when you get to the office, lock 'em up."

"All right," the doctor said, taking the key. "What're you going to do?"

"Well; you see; those folks're expecting the sheriff to ride in with whatever he's got. So I'll ride in—with a dead man and a badly wounded man, and they'll crowd up and I'll talk to 'em while you're locking up the live ones—then I'll come to the jailhouse and we'll have accomplished what we want to accomplish." The grey-level eyes went to the doctor's face. "Good luck, Pat. Get going."

While Nolan and Doctor Pat were breaking off, westerly, the sheriff sat his horse beside Eliza Ward's wagon listening to the clamour of townsmen. He sighed, pushed back his hat and looked down at the woman.

"Odd thing about people, ma'm. First, they want strong law enforcement—then—when they get it, they think they can enforce the law better than professional lawmen."

"It will be more odd," Mrs. Ward said crisply, "if they

don't take Sheridan out of my wagon and hang him."

"No; they won't hang a dying man."

She looked up at him. "He's not dying."

Mike smiled thinly. "Maybe he isn't, but you'd better show him how to act like he is before we drive through that crowd, because if he looks healthy, they just might lynch him, at that."

"And what will you do if they try to take him?"

"Let them have him, ma'm. Sheridan's not worth getting you and Will, and myself, killed over, and that's what it'll take to keep them back if they're fired up enough."

Eliza Ward's hands whitened around the lines she held, but no fear showed on her face. Mike drew back and edged around until he was beside Will Herman.

"Looks like some of your customers, Will."

Herman's face was grey in the moonlight. "I hope not," he said fervently. He looked out where Pat and Nolan had disappeared. "Will it work, Sheriff?" Then, before Mike could reply, Herman thrust out an arm and said, "Two riders coming." There was a tightness to the words.

Mike loped ahead to meet the oncoming riders. When he recognised them, he twisted in the saddle and signalled for Will and Eliza Ward to start moving.

Hugh Grant's heavy face was worried looking. Before he greeted the sheriff or asked about the fight he said: "Mob in town, Mike. They're talking hangrope."

"I guessed as much from the sound and the lanterns." Mike looked at the second rider. "How're things otherwise, Thomas?"

The deputy spread his hands and made a wry face. "There are no other things, *jefe*—only this talk of hanging whoever you bring in."

"Well; that show's confidence anyway. How'd they know I'd bring in anyone at all?"

Velarde shrugged and Hugh Grant, looking down into the wagon with a scowl, said: "Is that one of 'em?"

"Yes."

"Is he dead?"

Eliza Ward slowed the wagon long enough to reply to Grant. "No, he's not dead—but he's certainly scairt to death."

"I'll go on ahead a short ways," the sheriff said. "You fellers ride on each side of the wagon. Will; they won't bother you and the led-horse, so just keep moving. You too, Mrs. Ward—don't stop until you're at the jailhouse, even if you have to bump a few people."

They moved out, pushing closer to the dancing lanterns and the low throb of voices, and when they were close enough, the sheriff estimated the crowd's numbers. There were at least fifty men, and a number of them weaved unsteadily on their feet. He made an annoyed sound at that, then the mob was surging out to meet him.

CHAPTER SEVEN

FALSE DAWN was brightening the eastern sky when Antonia heard the slam of hastening boots on the plankwalk, the quick cry of men's voices, rising clear in the new day, and she got up, dressed, put a shawl around her shoulders although it was warm out, and left the house hurrying west on Grant Street as far as the corner, where Front Street ran north and south.

There, the sound of men rushing together was louder, and the cries had given way before a steady throb of sound, voices blurring together. Over by the jailhouse she saw massive Hugh Grant and the slim Mexican deputy standing in dark shadows, talking. A moment later they started toward the liverybarn, and until they passed *Carleton's Casino* she was not sure they were not going to join the crowd collecting there.

Across the road men called to Grant. He looked around but did not change course. Antonia watched him turn into the barn beside the deputy, then her attention was caught by the swelling group of men down by the *Casino*. A tall man was waving a rope and laughing. Others were saying his name and talking about hanging someone. Not until she strained to hear words instead of sounds, did she know that someone had seen the sheriff returning with prisoners; then the things she saw made sense.

Dawn was close and a soft, pale light filled the world as Antonia made her way as far north as the emporium, and stood back in the recessed doorway watching. Then she saw the riders for the first time. Sheriff Mike was in the lead. Behind him was an old wagon with two men on either side of it. Her breath caught short; the driver of the wagon was a woman. Beyond her, leading what at first glance appeared to be a pack-horse, was a fourth horseman. He was sitting bolt upright in the saddle, unnaturally stiff and apprehensive looking. The crowd of men converged on Sheriff Mike, and someone, out ahead, spoke in sharp surprise so that the sound carried over the low murmur. "By God he's even got a woman!"

The crowd grew nearly silent. The same strong voice said, "Both of 'em dead, Sheriff?" And Mike's reply carried back.

"Only one, Dade. The other one's only half-dead."

Mike's horse crowded people aside. Antonia watched the way he forced a passage for the wagon, then a raw curse sounded and the sheriff's voice, turned hard, cut it short. "Get out of the way. You'll have plenty of chances to look at 'em later on. Get back."

The crowd split. It was nearly silent now. Antonia saw the man with the rope looking after the wagon, standing in dark dust, undecided. A drunk cowboy approached him and his voice sounded loud in the silence.

"We can still hang him—if he ain't too dead—can't we?"

No one replied and the man with the rope turned away.

When Mike swung in at the hitchrail in front of the jailhouse, he looked long at the newly lit lamp inside, then he looped his reins methodically and went back to the wagon and helped the woman down. Antonia squinted for a closer look, but all she could make out was that the woman was thin, and that her hair was pulled severely away from a centre parting and bunched at the back of her head. Then the door of the office opened and two men emerged. One, Antonia recognised as Doctor Pat. The other one she did not see clearly until he moved out of the press of people, moving toward the led-horse. It was Deputy Velarde.

The crowd watched them carry both the dead man and the injured outlaw inside, and as silent men thickened, they hindered Antonia's view. Then Mike was filling the doorway with lamp light outlining him from behind, and he was speaking to the men in the roadway.

"Go get a drink," he said to them. "If I get a chance I'll join you later."

He closed the door softly, and the crowd stood a moment, before it began to thread its way back toward the *Casino*. Once more the discord of voices sounded clear in the freshening light as the men trooped off, and when the last one was gone, Antonia came out of the shadows, crossed the road and rapped softly on the office door.

Mike opened it. There was a dark frown on his face. He contemplated her a moment in surprise, then swung the door open and stepped back. She entered and stopped short. Three guns were trained on her. Their holders looked as startled as the sheriff had been. They holstered the weapons, looking at her impassively. Finally, Hugh Grant spoke:

"Toni . . . What you doin' out this hour of the night, anyway?"

Mike took her arm and led her toward the wall bench. The unattractive woman who was bent over beside Doctor Pat at a cot near the stove, straightened up and looked around. Her eyes were cool and authoritative. "Well;" she said to Will Herman who was standing beside the stove next to the saddlemaker, "Don't just stand there—make some coffee."

Mike took up a key off the table and went through the door which led to his cell-block beyond the office. Tom Velarde trailed after him. While they were gone Householder's barman stoked up a fire and made coffee. He was rinsing tin cups in a water-bucket when the sheriff returned, walking behind a faded, anxious looking, thin man.

Mrs. Ward shot her husband a long look, then smiled at him. Her disillusioned face lit up from within. Antonia thought it a rare and beautiful smile. Doctor Pat rummaged in a coat pocket and produced a key which he handed to the thin woman.

"My office is across the road. Just inside the door is my bag. On the same table is a medicine chest. Bring back what we'll need here."

As the woman went toward the door she looked at the faded man. "Come on," she said. "I'll need help carrying things."

The man swung toward Mike and the sheriff's eyes twinkled from a tired face. He jerked his head toward the door without speaking and the man went out.

When the coffee was ready Will Herman courteously took the first cup to Antonia. When Mike got the second cup he crossed to the bench and sank down beside her watching his brother work over the wounded man. He thrust his legs far out and sipped the coffee with obvious enjoyment. Antonia turned to him.

"Weren't there others?" she asked.

"Yes; there were four. One's dead, that's another one, and the other two are locked up in the cages."

"But I only saw two."

"Pat took the other two around the back way. I didn't want the mob to get them."

Nolan and Herman were talking together over by the stove. Finally the bartender crossed to Mike and said, "Fred and I'll go on home now if you don't need us any more."

Mike nodded. "Sure; and thanks, boys." Then, as the

men were leaving, he said: "Nolan; I'd like to see you this afternoon."

"I'll come by after noon, Sheriff."

Mike watched the men leave, then he got up and barred the door behind them. Hugh Grant saw him do it and raised his eyebrows. As the sheriff was returning to the bench he said, "Folks'll find out about the other two." He sank down next to Antonia again and finished the coffee.

An abrupt knock on the door brought them all around. Mike opened it to admit the Wards. As Eliza went toward the cot the sheriff caught her husband's arm.

"See anything out there like a mob forming?"

Ward shook his head. "No; the road's deserted."

"Good." Mike continued to gaze at the homesteader a moment. "Ward; the liverybarn in town here needs a man to run it. 'Want to try it?"

Ward's face softened. "My wife told me about that while we were at the doctor's office. I'd like nothing better than the chance, Sheriff."

"Good. I'll see about it later on."

"Sheriff; I want to thank you for what you've done tonight—or last night, rather."

Mike's gaze lingered. "Feel grateful do you? Well; you can repay me easy, Ward."

"Name it, Sheriff."

"I've got an idea in the back of my mind. I'll let you know about it after I've had my ear to the ground."

Mike went back beside Antonia and Ed Ward watched him a moment with a puzzled expression, then he joined Hugh Grant and the others over by the cot.

"I'd better walk you home," the sheriff said to Antonia.

"Isn't there something I can do here?"

Mike was leaning forward to arise when he said, "Yes, there is; you can let the Wards stay with you for a few days, until they get things worked out."

She arose beside him. "I'd be glad to have them, Mike."

As he was passing through the door Mike said, "Tom; bar the door after me, and keep it barred from now on. I'll be back directly." The grey eyes went to Doctor Pat's back. "How's he look, Pat?"

Without looking around the sheriff's brother replied: "Not too bad, Mike. He'll feel worse for a week or so, but he'll be on the mend."

Mike nodded to Hugh Grant and closed the door softly.

Outside, Vacaville was coming to life. People were gathered in front of the stores talking. They watched Sheriff Mike and Antonia Parker cross the roadway and fade from sight down Grant Street. Sunlight shone strong and warm, and Mike felt it soaking into his body. He walked in stony silence as far as Antonia's porch, and there he halted with a wide yawn and a grin.

"Tired," he said. "Toni . . . don't carry that gun."

She looked at him in surprise, and over a considerable interval she was silent. Then: "All right, I won't."

"Shooting's a man's job. Besides," Mike said, "those little guns aren't very accurate."

"I wanted to end it . . . I started it."

Mike put his back against the warming wood of the house. His head was dropped and his eyes held to her face with a considering attention. She stood by the door meeting his glance, lips faintly parted and a solemn gravity looking out of her eyes.

"I've done a terrible thing, Mike."

"I won't disagree," he answered. "But no one could convince me you knew how it would work out. Anyway, people don't do much that's worthwhile without first making mistakes."

"Now there are five people dead instead of one. You were right—what you said about killings, Mike."

He reached out, touched her cheek with one hand, let his fingers go lower, to her shoulder, and lie there. "The thing to remember, Toni, is that the world doesn't end because folks die—or make mistakes. It only ends for them when they repeat their mistakes, or die themselves."

Her eyes clouded. "I don't understand, exactly."

"I mean, learn to live with what you've lost—Reed Benton—don't make things worse by avenging a memory."

She looked down and put her hand on the door latch. "I think," she said slowly, and without looking at him, "that I have learned that already." Then she raised her head. "A person can recover from loss very quickly—when there is something else to hold them, Mike."

"Like hate?"

"Not exactly. That's only a part of it." She was shaking her head. "The rest is not so easy to define." Her eyes cleared and she raised the latch. "Let me fix you some breakfast."

He hesitated, watching the faint beat of pulse in her throat, then he pushed off the siding. "I'd better not, Toni; not today."

She searched his face. "There is going to be more trouble, isn't there?"

"I'd like to think there isn't, but I'm not that confident. The thing that surprised me when we rode in this morning, was that the men from Skull Valley weren't waiting, too."

"Oh," Antonia said softly. "Of course. I guess I'd forgotten. There were stories around town last night about that. Are they true, Mike?"

"They probably are. Jack Arbuckle and his father were killed."

"He killed Smith, didn't he?"

Mike shook his head. "No, he didn't—but it didn't make any difference to Slidell's crew."

She watched his face and let the latch fall. There was a sudden warm expression in her eyes. "You're tired, aren't you; why don't you at least let me fix you some coffee?"

He smiled. "I think it's going to take something stronger than coffee to keep me going today." He turned away.

"Mike?"

She went across to him and leaned forward, the jut of her bosom lying firm against his shirt, and she kissed him full on the mouth. The bite of fingernails along his arms went deep with sharp pressure, then she moved back and dropped her arms, and there was neither embarrassment nor confusion in her unwavering eyes.

"Come back tonight, if you can—and—please Mike—be careful."

He waited until she was gone, then went down the walk to the dust of Grant Street and turned west, toward the heart of town. All his weariness had dropped away. At the doorway of Vacaville's solitary attorney, John Hunt, he paused a moment, then entered the office and saw the quick look a dark-headed man behind a roll-top desk cast upwards at him.

"Hello, John."

" 'Sheriff. You made quite a catch, I hear."

"About average," Mike replied with a twinkle. The lawyer laughed. "Say John; did Reed Benton leave a will?"

"He did, and I intend to file it within the next day or two; why do you ask?"

"Who got the liverybarn?"

"The liverybarn, together with its chattels and appurtenances, and everything else he had, goes to Antonia Parker."

Mike drew himself up and turned toward the door. "Thanks," he said to the attorney. "That simplifies something for me. I've got an experienced liveryman on my hands, and he needs work."

"To run the barn?"

"Yes."

"Good. Go see Antonia. She'll need someone now that Hank Hubbel's gone." The lawyer's smile came up faintly. "It's a poor wind that doesn't blow some good, Mike. Vacaville benefited from the killing when Hubbel left."

Mike left the office and turned right, toward Charley Householder's saloon. He had to pass *Carleton's Casino* to get there, and after he'd gone by someone called to him from the doorway of the *Casino.* He stopped and turned. It was Carl Braun from Skull Valley—whose mother was an Indian. Braun was short and powerful. His face was flat, round, and very swarthy. He sauntered along the plankwalk without taking his eyes off the sheriff's face. When he spoke, finally, he stopped and stood wide-legged.

"There was four of 'em, Sheriff. Four—not two."

Mike looked steadily into the black eyes. "That's right," he said coldly, "there were four of 'em."

"You only brought back two. Where are the others?"

"What business is it of yours?"

Braun's voice jumped at him. "The same as anyone else from the Valley—I'm makin' it my business."

The sheriff studied Braun's face a moment, through an interval of silence. "Have you been drinking?" he asked.

Braun's face darkened and his eyes became pinpoints of fire. "Don't change the subject on me, McMahon. Where are them other two murderers!"

"Safe and sound."

Braun's thin lips drew back from his teeth. "Feelin' pretty cocky today, ain't you?"

Anger burst and blood flooded into the sheriff's face. "Why you scurvy little whelp," he said in a flat, hard tone, "When the day comes I have to answer questions from the likes of you, I'll hang up the badge. Now you get on your horse and get out of town."

Braun stood stock still; only a ripple of muscle along his jaw showed that he had heard. The sheriff, watching closely, saw the 'breed's shoulders sag the smallest bit.

"Go ahead, Braun. You've needed killing for a long time. Go ahead and draw it."

Braun did not go for the gun he wore. Instead, he spun on his heel and walked away. Mike watched him until he was well down the plankwalk, then he resumed his way toward Householder's. When he got there and was pushing in past the doors, the sound of a running horse brought him back around. Carl Braun was quirting his mount at every jump, riding south.

Mike went to the bar with a bitter, drawn-down expression on his face. Hugh Grant, who was sitting at a table, called his name softly. Seated across from Grant was Amos Hatfield, the restaurant owner, his fat bulk nearly as great as Grant's own fat. Mike took a beer over to the table, scarcely looked at Hatfield, nodded to Hugh and dropped down.

"Amos's been telling me the Skull Valleyers are in town, Mike," Grant said.

"One just left—Carl Braun. I ordered him out of town."

Hatfield's eyebrows lifted and his small, deep-set eyes widened. "I seen three of 'em ride in early, Mike."

"What of it?" the sheriff asked irritably.

"They'll be after your prisoners," Hatfield said, and leaned upon the table to make his whispered words carry. "Folks know you got all four of them outlaws in your jail." Hatfield leaned back triumphantly. "The best way to keep a secret in Vacaville is to tell it first."

The sheriff gazed at Hugh Grant. "Yeah," he said dourly. "And if folks don't know for sure, they can make up a good lie to fill in with."

"Well," Hatfield expostulated. "You got 'em, haven't you?"

"You know, Amos; I just asked Carl Braun what business that was of his."

Hatfield's jowls shook, and his voice turned whining. "Well hell, Sheriff; I'm just interested is all. If there's goin' to be battle right here in town, us merchants got a right to know."

"How the devil do I know if there's going to be a fight, Amos?"

"You know—if you got two unhurt outlaws in the jail-house."

"You just said I had 'em. Now you're asking me *if* I have 'em." Mike drank off the beer and put the glass down squarely. "Tell you what, Amos; you better get along to your cafe and mind your cooking. When my deputy comes around for three trays of grub instead of one, you'll know I've got the other two locked up—and you can spread the word."

Hatfield frowned at McMahon, then got up and left. For a while neither Grant nor the sheriff spoke. Grant drained the glass in his hand and peered in at the dregs. "You can't keep a secret long," he said, set the glass down and pushed it aside. "Like Amos said—folks'll know, Mike." The puffy eyes looked out shrewdly. "Then what?"

"Then I go right on keeping them locked up."

"Well; much as I dislike saying so, Amos was right about there being a scrap if the Skull Valley folk hear you got 'em."

"They'll hear quick enough. Braun didn't ride hard out of Vacaville just because I sent him off. He knows I've got them locked up."

"Uh huh; now they'll be riding into town."

Mike looked across the table. "Worried, Hugh?" he asked.

Irritation creased Hugh Grant's face. "I'd be an idiot if I wasn't worried. You would be, too. Why don't you send Slidell and the Mex over to Junction City while there's still time?"

Mike leaned back and yawned. "Because," he replied wearily, "they'd get them out of the Junction City jailhouse even quicker than they will here. Folks at Junction City don't want a part of Vacaville's troubles, Hugh; they've got enough of their own."

Grant studied Mike through a considerable silence and afterwards put his glance on the empty glasses. "I've got a duty, too." he said heavily. "I've got to think of the town and the folks here."

Mike's attention centred on the big man. "Being a town councilman must be pretty rugged," he said with unmistakable irony. "But I don't think anyone'll kill you over it."

"Meaning what?"

"Meaning they might kill me—but until they do, those two killers stay in the jailhouse here."

"Well now, Mike, by golly; suppose the council orders you to get them out of town?"

"I'll take them out of town, Hugh, when I'm ordered to—but when I do that, I want your town council to know something: They won't just be sending Slidell and Belasco to their deaths, they'll be sending me too, because I'll fight to keep those men, and don't you forget it."

Sheriff Mike got up. Hugh Grant did not lift his eyes from the empty glasses as Mike crossed the room and left the cafe.

Outside, sunlight burned against the earth and waves of heat shimmered upwards, layer upon layer of them. Down the road Doctor Pat and Eliza Ward were crossing through the dust. They were engaged in conversation and looked neither right nor left. Nearer, a buckboard wheeled into the overhang-shade and a cowman got down and pulled angrily at a saddle with a broken cinch and torn rigging. Mike watched him limp purposefully toward Nolan's saddle shop. Across the way, and up a piece, where the maw of the liverybarn gaped darkly, two riders were squatting in the shade whittling through a desultory conversation; both their heads were down, faces shielded by dusty big hats.

Someone shuffled up behind the sheriff and mumbled at him. He turned. It was "G. B." Buckholz, the livery hostler. He was carrying a bucket of beer which he balanced gently by a bale to keep the liquid from sloshing out.

"Folks're gettin' edgy, Sheriff," he said softly, pale eyes solemn.

"You, too, G.B.?"

The holster made a wry face and shook his head. "Naw; 'feller sees as many dreams turn to sand as I've seen, Sheriff, don't nothing worry him a hell of a lot." G.B. held the bucket up. "Care for a sip?"

"No thanks; just had one. Hubbel come back yet?"

Another head-shake. "Nope. I don't look for him to, either."

"Think he's scaired out?"

"Not exactly. I think he cleaned out the strongbox."

Mike's glance sharpened. "At the liverybarn?"

"Yup."

"You sure, G.B.?"

"Well, Sheriff; I put some money in, couple hours before he hightailed it. Half an hour later I went to put in some more—and the box was empty. Now Reed ain't around to take it and I sure didn't—so that leaves Hank, don't it?"

"How much did he get?"

Buckholz moved to shield the beer from the sun's direct rays. "Ain't been no deposits made at the stage company's safe since Reed got it. I'd guess there was about eleven hundred dollars in there." Buckholz fidgeted. "I reckon the new owner'll blame me and I'll be packin' down the trail, too, pretty quick now. Well; them things happen, don't they?"

Mike had known Buckholz since he'd come to Vacaville six years before. He knew him to be an honest man. He said: "Do you know who the new owner is, G.B.?"

"Nope. Probably someone from back East."

"It's someone right here in town, and I'll lay you odds they won't fire you. Want to bet on it?"

Buckholz forgot the beer momentarily. "Who is it, Sheriff?"

Mike grinned. "Can't say. It's up to Reed's lawyer to do that. But there'll be a new manager at the barn pretty quick now, if the cards fall right, and I think you two'll get along fine."

G.B. looked dubious. "Will he like beer?"

"I think so. And maybe a little poker during the hot time of day, too. He looks like a man who plays a little."

"Ahhh; you know him? Who is he?"

"Feller named Ward; does that tell you anything?"

"Ward?" Buckholz said, puckering up his face. "No; 'don't believe I know anyone hereabouts named Ward."

"I was sure you didn't, G.B.; that's why I told you."

"Sheriff . . . ?"

But Mike was moving along the walk toward a small knot of men standing in the shade across from the jailhouse. He did not look back.

The men looked up when Sheriff Mike appeared. They seemed embarrassed. Mike patted a big, fat man on the shoulder and said: "Make it good, Amos," and went on by.

Dade Carleton was striding north along the walk carrying a bundle from the emporium. When he came abreast of the sheriff he halted. The scar on his left cheek, crescent-shaped, shone pale and oily. "Hear now that you got 'em all, Mike. That you tricked us this morning and snuck the two unhurt ones into the jailhouse the back way."

"You sure can hear things around Vacaville, can't you," Mike replied, with unusual warmth and geniality. "The trouble is—you never know whether they're true or not—do you?"

Carleton's face coloured. He stood fast for a moment then edged on around the sheriff and toward his saloon without another word.

Mike stepped down into the dust and crossed to the shade of the jailhouse overhang. From there he looked back up the road. Men were talking here and there, a brace of faded cowboys trotted down through the dust heading for *Carleton's Casino*, and the clear peal of steel striking an anvil at Grant's Forge rose flute-like in the stifling air. Vacaville had never looked so peaceful to the sheriff; so languidly pleasant. He continued to gaze outward a moment longer, then he turned toward the barred door and raised his fist to knock. There was a sardonic expression around his eyes.

Chapter Eight

Tom Velarde was alone in the office when Sheriff Mike returned. He was relieved to see who had thumped on the door.

When Mike entered and Velarde barred the door after

him, the sheriff asked: "How's Sheridan?"

"He drinks a lot of water," the deputy said, noncommittally.

Mike crossed to the cot and stood there looking down at the grey, slack face. "Sheridan?" The sunken eyes opened. "How do you feel?"

"Like the last rose of summer," the wounded man answered in a voice gone deep and thick. "You got Curt and Dominguez locked up?"

"Yeah . . . That was a senseless thing you fellers did. I reckon you know that now, don't you?"

"No . . . Someone bushwhacked Shiloh."

"But not Arbuckle, Sheridan—it was a man named Locke Hibbard."

Sheridan's eyes clung dryly to Mike's face. " 'You sure about that?"

"Yes."

"All right, Sheriff; we'll get him."

Mike tilted back his hat. "I doubt it. Like I told Slidell when we were bringing you boys in—our circuit judge's short on patience and long on rope."

The wounded man licked his lips and stared at the ceiling. After a time he said, "Your judge's going to have to rattle his hocks if he aims to hang me—I won't be around a lot longer, Sheriff."

"You'll make it. The doctor said you would."

Mike turned away, got the keys to the cell-block and passed from the outer office. When Slidell and Belasco heard him coming, they looked up from where they were resting on straw pallets within the same strap-steel cage. Belasco smiled disarmingly without speaking, but Curt

Slidell's gaze was cold. "When you goin' to feed us?" He demanded of Mike.

"I've got a little problem there," Mike answered. "If I send out for trays, the cafeman'll know I've got you in here. He'll spread the word around town."

"What of it?"

"As long as folks aren't sure you're here, Slidell, they won't get up a lynch-mob."

Slidell frowned. "You mean they don't know, already?"

"They aren't sure," Mike stated. "Now—if you boys like Mexican cooking, I can send out for grub from the Mex restaurant in Old Town."

"Food's food," Slidell growled. "And somethin' else we want, too—a lawyer."

Mike considered the gunman a moment, then he said: "Aren't you interested in Sheridan—whether he lives or not?"

"It won't make any difference in what happens to us, will it—then we aren't interested."

Mike heard Velarde's big Chihuahua spurs ringing and looked around. The deputy motioned toward the outer door when he spoke: "The saddlemaker is out there. Shall I let him in?"

Mike moved forward. "Yeah."

Fred Nolan had shaved. His lantern-jaw, long nose and rather prominent eyes, shone from a recent scrubbing. When Mike came into the office he nodded to him. "You wanted to see me?"

Mike tossed the keys on the table and pulled his hat forward. "Take a walk to Old Town with me. We can talk on the way." From the doorway Mike said: "Tom; keep the door barred and don't let anyone in. I'll send some food up for you and our guests."

Nolan and McMahon crossed through the dust of the roadway, anglingly. As they walked the sheriff talked, and when they reached the saddle shop and paused outside it, Nolan was nodding.

"I'll co-operate," he said. "Just let me know when you want me."

Mike put a big hand lightly on Nolan's sleeve, then let it fall away. He resumed his way toward the Mexican section alone. Behind him, Fred Nolan stood in the doorway of his establishment looking out where the heat droned on; out where the barest trickle of lethargic traffic moved, then he ducked into the coolness of the shop and was lost to sight.

Mex town was even more bare of life than Front Street was. Here and there a black-eyed child watched the big lawman pass with wide eyes. Tattered, soiled remnants of the fiesta lay underfoot, and over by the barbecue pits a number of scavenging dogs, lean and sharp-eyed, sniffed for offal.

As soon as Epifanio Chavez saw Sheriff Mike enter his darkened, empty cafe, he came forward with a long, gloomy face.

"*Buenas dias, amigo.*"

"Howdy 'Pifas. Send someone to the jailhouse with four trays of food, will you? And 'Pifas—be sure they go down the back-alley."

Epifanio nodded, black, velvetty eyes unmoving. "Then it is true that you have the others, no?"

"It's true—but I'd like to keep it quiet as long as I can."

Chavez made a gesture. "I will take the food myself, and

no one will know what I am carrying. Trust me, *Señor.*"

Mike sat down on the counter-bench. "I do; that's why I came here."

Chavez made two cups of bitter chocolate and put one in front of the sheriff. He leaned against a food table, covered against the flies with a white cloth, and held the second cup in a dark hand.

"Carlos Fortier and Bruce Martin are in town, *jefe.* I saw them earlier, at the liverybarn."

"I know. I saw them, too, squatting in the shade with their hats over their faces, whittling and talking like they had nothing on their minds."

Chavez sipped the chocolate, his eyes hard on Mike's face. "Carl Braun was also in town, but he left." The Mexican's voice was strong with meaning.

Mike drank the chocolate and put the cup down empty. "Yeah. Carl's gone to round up the rest of the Skull Valley men," he said, getting up. "Maybe you were right, 'Pifas."

"*Señor?*"

"The night you and that rancher were talking about cancelling the fiesta—about there being trouble in the wind."

Chavez's eyes brightened a little. "I remember, of a certainty, *jefe;* still, a man takes small pleasure in being right about such things." Chavez put his cup down. "And *jefe;* what of Tomas Velarde?"

"What of him?"

A shrug. "The Mexican settlement cannot go on paying his wages. It was only for the fiesta, you will remember."

"Oh. The town council has agreed to keep him on as my deputy, 'Pifas. You folks won't have to pay anything—not even for the fiesta."

Chavez looked pleased, and yet he also looked surprised. "It is a good thing. Tomas is a fine boy. But *jefe;* he is a Mexican."

"No one said he wasn't a Mexican."

"But there is feeling . . . not between old friends like you and me, I know—but this is a natural thing with the others of our races. You understand."

Mike nodded. "Maybe folks will find out there isn't much difference, 'Pifas. Maybe they'll accept Tomas as a good lawman."

Chavez was doubtful. "*Señor* Grant?" he said softly. "We have both known him a long time. He does not like Mexicans."

Mike's eyes became ironically amused. "You'd be surprised, 'Pifas—it was Hugh Grant who agreed to keep Tom as my deputy."

Chavez's eyebrows went up, then he, too, smiled. "A miracle, *jefe.* An old dog does not usually learn new tricks."

"Before the week's out," Mike replied, walking toward the door, "I think a lot of old dogs are going to learn some new tricks. *Adios.*"

Chavez's reply was soft. "Go with God," he said—"*Vaya con Dios*"—as the sheriff left the cafe and bright sunlight splashed upwards against him from the soiled dust of the crooked roadway.

Vacaville, at mid-day, was usually somnolent. Today it was no different. Mike strolled south along the plankwalk feeling for tension; there was none. He looked over the door at Charley Householder's saloon, and got a listless wave from Will Herman. At the *Casino*, too, there were only a sprinkling of customers. Farther along, down by the lawyer's office, two cowboys sat on a bench, silent and drowsing. Mike recognised them both but passed by without looking down or speaking. They turned their heads to watch him, then one drew out a gold watch, snapped open the front, gazed at it a moment, then closed it and pocketed it.

" 'Be another couple hours," he said, and his relaxed companion nodded.

"Can't push a horse too hard on a day like this. If he don't get back with the others till night it'll be better anyway."

The first cowboy, still watching the sheriff's retreating back, said: "You afraid of him, Carlos?"

For a moment the dark-faced, sparse rider didn't reply, then he said: " 'You ever seen him in action? Well, I have; an' I got lots of respect for him."

The lingering gaze held to Mike's back until he stepped off the plankwalk into the hot dust of Grant Street, heading east toward Antonia Parker's house.

The heat was pressing down, its glare, like its intensity, oppressive and stifling. Windless air hung invisibly solid and as Mike went up to the porch of Antonia's house, he leaned into it.

The girl answered his second knock, then moved aside as he entered. When he looked kitchenward at the sound of voices, she said: "The Wards."

"That's what I came to talk to you about."

"Sit down, Mike."

He waited until she sat, then sank down gratefully, breathing deeply of the room's coolness behind drawn blinds.

"Have you seen John Hunt yet?"

"The lawyer? No; should I?"

"You're Reed's heir, Toni. He left you the liverybarn."

Antonia looked astonished. "The liverybarn . . . ?"

"Yes. What I wanted to talk about was a replacement for Hank Hubbel."

Antonia hadn't recovered from her surprise. She nodded perfunctorily. "Yes?"

"Mr. Ward."

"Oh." The girl smoothed her dark skirt. Above it, a white, severely cut bodice with the throat lying open, swelled with the strong jut of bosom. The lovely eyes framed with a sweep of long lashes held to Mike's face. "Is he qualified?" She flicked one hand gently. "I don't know anything about liverybarns, Mike."

"His wife says he is, and I've got a feeling about him, Toni. Why not give him a chance?"

"Of course. Shall I call him? He's eating in the kitchen."

Mike got up, his gaze both hungry and gentle. "No; just tell him to go down and take over. G.B. can show him the routine."

She stood, and in the shaded room her hair lay in a dull way about her face, softly inviting. "But why me? Why did Reed do that?"

Mike hunched his shoulders and let them sag. "He loved you, Toni. I can't think of a better reason."

"But he had relatives in Missouri. He told me about them."

"Sure; but blood isn't thicker than love. Besides, after Reed's folks died in the epidemic of '76, those people in Missouri couldn't find room for him. I know; he told

130

me about it."

Antonia's face became troubled. She looked down. "I don't think I ought to take the barn, though."

"Why not? He left it to you—he wanted you to have it, Toni."

"Because—well—it'd be like taking something under false pretences."

The sheriff was puzzled and it showed. When the girl looked up she saw his expression and moved several steps closer to him.

"I—don't think I'd have married Reed."

"Everyone else thought you would. It was sort of taken for granted around town."

"Well; I might have. I don't know. I suppose if all this hadn't happened I would have. But now—today—I couldn't, Mike."

"Toni, I don't understand you."

"I wasn't in love with him."

"But you—"

"I thought I was. I was sure of it, Mike. Then, after he was killed—after it was all over . . ." She kept her face lifted toward his but their eyes did not meet. "This is difficult to say Mike. Afterwards—something came to me—something far greater than the feeling I'd had for Reed. Do you understand?"

"No," Mike replied, with hesitancy in his voice. "I don't think I do."

"Well; maybe it was because I was afraid I wasn't ever going to get married, Mike. Anyway; what I felt for Reed wasn't at all what I feel for you." She was looking at him with great intensity, great anxiety, and when he did not speak she put a hand on his arm. "That was a terrible thing to say, wasn't it?"

He took her hand in one of his and reached for the other hand. "It's a wonderful thing to say, Toni. It's something like what's been inside me since the night I walked you home from the fiesta—only I reckon it comes easier for a woman to put a name to that feeling, than it does to a man."

She saw the quick pull of colour into his cheeks and the naked showing of expression in his eyes, and because of them she could not take a deep breath. She wanted him to go on talking, to break the awkward strangeness between them, but he became silent.

Then small, brisk footfalls came to them and they felt a third presence. The moment was destroyed; he let her hands drop away, and while her eyes clung wistfully to his face, she saw him incline his head; saw the mask of calm acceptance descend and hide the other things which had been on his face and in his eyes, then he was speaking.

"'Afternoon, Mrs. Ward. I guess you can send your husband 'round to the barn, the new owner's agreed to put him on."

Eliza Ward had not always been drab, thin, and colourless. Her eyes shifted slightly from Mike's flushed face to the fullness of Antonia's back, and when she spoke there was a deep remembering mellowness in her tones.

"You are a good man, Sheriff. I could bite my tongue off for the things I said—out there."

The mood was dead, the moment gone forever. Antonia turned. "He's also a persuasive man, Eliza," she said with forced lightness. "Reed Benton left me the liverybarn in his will."

Eliza Ward's gaze lingered on the girl's face. Her voice thickened and a hot dryness burned at her eyes. "I'll never forget either of you. Believe me I won't. And neither will Ed."

"Well," the sheriff said, moving to pick up his hat from the table. "I expect I'd better be getting back uptown." He held the hat in both hands looking past Antonia. "Maybe Ed could walk uptown with me."

"I'll get him." Eliza Ward turned swiftly away, thankful for an excuse to escape the room. In the kitchen she spoke swiftly to her husband, and when he arose from the table, she lay a detaining hand upon his shoulder. "Just for a minute—stay in here." She turned away from the puzzled look on her husband's face, and went to the stove. "I'll tell you when to go, Ed."

Mike's gaze moved over Toni's face. She saw the interest there; the growing intensity in his eyes, and she moved quickly forward, seeking his mouth with her lips, running her arms up around his shoulders to the back of his neck, and pressing downward, then, with the hard bursts of his breath on her face, she moved rapidly away, her own breathing pushing outward.

"Can you describe that feeling, Mike?"

He shook his head without speaking.

"That's what I meant—I never felt that for Reed. I'm ashamed of myself—ashamed to say such a thing. But I'm glad I feel that way now, because if it had come after Reed and I were married—I don't know what I'd have done."

Ed Ward came through the kitchen door, his head up and his eyes reaching across the room for the sheriff's face. He smiled at Antonia without seeing anything in her expression, crossed to the door and held it open for the sheriff to pass through, then he closed it.

Ward felt a strangeness in the big man beside him; he made no attempt to hold a conversation until they turned north at the intersection of Grant and Front streets and got onto the rough board walkway. Then he said: "I'm forever beholden to you and your brother, Sheriff."

Over an interval of walking the sheriff was silent. He did not speak until they were scuffing across the road through the glittering dust, then his words ran out easily as he explained how Ed Ward could repay him. At first the liveryman was startled, then he became worried, but by the time they were at the barn, his mouth had gone flat with resolve, and determination lay in his eyes.

"You tell me when and how," he said, "And I'll do my damndest."

Mike slapped him on the back, introduced him to G.B. and returned to the roadway with the echo of conversation following him from the barn's alleyway. It was rewarding to know you had taken a misfit off the desert; few men belonged out there, and for those who did not, the desert reserved a particular brand of torture.

He went south as far as the jailhouse, but he did not enter. There was an old bench beneath the wooden awning several feet farther along; he sat down upon it and made a cigarette, looking out into the glare from narrowed eyes, seeing nothing really, but feeling much.

Hugh Grant came out of *Householder's Saloon*, puckered his face against the glare, looked at a gold pocket watch, then threw a long glance up and down the roadway while he tucked the timepiece away. He cut straight across the road and turned south, his weight making the boards groan and buckle. When he was near enough he spoke out: "Where you been, Mike? There was a travelling man through a little while back from Tucson."

Mike looked up. "What about it? Did he break the law?"

Grant dropped down on the bench with a headshake. "No; he had an interesting bit of news, though. Hank Hubbel's dead."

Mike's serene look vanished. "How?"

"Killed in a poker game yesterday."

"In Tucson?"

"Yes. Seems Hubbel lost over a thousand dollars and called some cowboy out. The cowboy killed him in the roadway with half the town lookin' on."

Mike went back to staring outward into the sunlight. "I guess he had more sand in his craw than I credited him with," he said. "That thousand was part of some eleven hundred he stole from the liverybarn."

"No," Grant said, twisting sideways with a grunt. "Is that why he left town in such a hurry?"

"That's part of it. The biggest part, I reckon." Mike was thoughtful. "I guess Hank's life wasn't worth much more than eleven hundred dollars, if that's what he sold it for."

Grant leaned back and let off a quiet sigh. "I never cared for Hubbel—but y'know, Mike—I never get over bein' shocked when someone gets killed. I never carried a gun, myself—well; not very often anyway—and maybe that's why it don't seem right to me that folks can go around shootin' other folks."

Mike was watching a distant dust-banner. He made no addition to the conversation, and after a moment Hugh

135

Grant fell silent. The stillness settled deeply along Front Street. A fringe-top buggy went by, spokes glistening, the driver's up-curling hatbrim pulled low to shade his eyes. Two boys and a bored dog passed, also; the intense, hard young voices contrasting with the dulling heat.

Grant swung his head toward a distant sound, and his eyes fell upon the sheriff's profile. His lips were gently set, showing gravity and strong will, and he, too, was running a long glance outward where the sound was. Then Grant's big bulk shook with a tremour and the big man drew up, gradually straighter, on the bench.

"Here it comes, Mike."

"Yeah," the sheriff's voice said softly. "I've been watching the dust."

"Can you make out how many?"

"Not yet."

Grant drew up still more, his face shining dully with sweat. "Dammit," he said in a hard burst of breath, then protest sounded in his words. "I wish I'd made the council order you to get 'em out of town, first."

"It wouldn't have done any good, Hugh. They'd have come anyway."

"But they wouldn't have torn up Vacaville."

The sheriff said nothing; he watched the twisting dust grow greater, then it hung there out over the plain, and below it a party of riders was fully visible, jogging steadily toward Vacaville, sunlight glinting off their bits and conchos, and gun butts.

"Ten of 'em," Grant said. "I recognise those two greys out front—George and Jess Pratly."

"The big chestnut with the flaxen mane and tail," the

sheriff said quietly. "That's Locke Hibbard."

Hugh groaned and swore a solid oath. "I *knew* this was goin' to happen—I *knew* it, Mike."

The sheriff got to his feet and went past Grant to the door of his office. He rapped gently and when Tomas Velarde opened up, Mike raised an arm and pointed out where the riders were. Velarde strained hard to see, then rigidity came into his stance and he looked quickly at the big man in front of him.

"*Ai Dios*—ten of them."

Mike edged past and closed the door, dropping the *tranca* into place. He stood with his back to it for a moment, then he moved toward the wall-rack, pulled the chain through the trigger-guards there, and began checking the loads of the Winchesters and shotguns.

A big fist struck the outer door and when Velarde hesitated, the sheriff spoke over his shoulder. "That's Hugh Grant; let him in."

Velarde stepped back as the fat man entered, then he lingered in the doorway looking out where the riders were scuffing dust as they came past the outlying shacks at the south end of Vacaville.

Grant stood beside Mike mopping at sweat on his neck with a limp handkerchief. "You could still get 'em out the back way," he said.

"Not a chance," the sheriff replied, replacing a gun in the rack and taking down another one. "Those Skull Valleyers can read more from the dust of running horses than you can from a book."

Grant's voice arose with desperation. "What are you going to do, then? You can't hope to hold this damned jailhouse."

Mike checked the last weapon and replaced it. He turned to face the blacksmith shop owner. "In a pinch I'll call on the townsmen, Hugh."

"Be sensible, Mike. You know damned well how they feel. They'll help the Skull Valleyers, if they help anyone at all."

"In that case," Sheriff Mike said, "I'll have to fall back on another idea."

Tom Velarde called from the outer office: "Sheriff; they are coming here—to the jailhouse."

Grant swore again, another blistering oath, then he fixed a long stare on the sheriff. "All right," he said after a moment. "I got confidence in you—but I don't know why. You're sure playing this hand like an idiot." He reached around Mike, toward the gun-rack. The sheriff pushed his arm aside.

"No need for that yet. Let's try palaver first."

"Now I know you're crazy," Grant spluttered, but he let the arm fall to his side.

Beyond the barred door there was the sound of many horses slowing. A moment later saddles creaked as men dismounted. When the hard slam of boots struck the plankwalk, the sheriff pointed to the wall bench. "Sit over there," he told Hugh Grant. "At the far end, near the door."

Grant moved away, his face as dark as thunder. Mike took down a loaded scatter-gun, crossed to the table and layed it there, quick to hand. When the gloved fist struck the door he looked at Velarde, whose thin, dark face was pale under the natural pigment.

"Stay where you are, Tom. You'll be behind them." Mike

nodded toward the bar across the door. "Let in the first two and no more." Velarde touched his gun-butt and the sheriff nodded.

When the door swung inward ten hard-bitten faces were beyond it staring in. The first three men were Jess and George Pratly and Locke Hibbard. Velarde motioned the Pratly's in and started to close the door. Sheriff Mike spoke:

"Let Hibbard in too."

For a moment after Velarde had closed the door behind Locke Hibbard, the last one through, it was quiet enough to hear a pin drop—then Hugh Grant cleared his throat with a suppressed rumble, and the Pratlys looked around at him. Grant returned their wide stare with narrowed eyes.

With the possible exception of the injured outlaw, every man in the sheriff's office had known the others at least ten years, and generally, much longer. But the years were forgotten and only bitterness and stony resolve showed now.

George Pratly, the younger brother, wore two guns, both lashed to his legs. He carried a carbine. His brother Jesse, a taciturn, bleak man, as grey and wily as an old wolf, wore only one sidearm and, like Locke Hibbard, he carried no rifle. Hibbard removed doeskin riding gloves with slow, deliberate motions, and his eyes did not leave the sheriff's face after he heard the door close behind him.

Hibbard was a flashy man in his early thirties. He was known as a good man with a gun; he was also known to possess a cold and calculating disposition. Sheriff Mike had known him since boyhood; he had never had occasion to run him out of town nor arrest him, but he had long ago recognised the inevitability of having to do both. Now, knowing Hibbard had ambushed Shiloh Smith, the sheriff's gaze lingered longest on him.

Beyond the door, and above the soft sound of shifting feet along the plankwalk, Mike could hear the quick, deep silence which had settled over Vacaville. He knew well what that stillness meant.

George Pratly moved finally, walking toward the cot by the stove. He stopped and looked down at Matthew Sheridan and his face was like granite. Jess, too, crossed to stand above the injured man, but Locke Hibbard cast only a casual glance toward the cot. He turned slowly, deliberately, and looked from Hugh Grant, motionless and watching on the bench, to Deputy Velarde, back by the door. Ultimately, his glance swept back to the sheriff, and for a long time it remained there.

Mike did not sit, although his chair was close behind; he waited. He did not believe the men from Skull Valley would attempt to take his prisoners yet, but that decision lay with them and he stood prepared to resist. It is possible that the Pratlys and Hibbard might have tried it, except that Sheriff Mike was not alone in the office, and very clearly both Velarde and Hugh Grant did not just happen to be in a flanking position.

CHAPTER NINE

WHEN the elder Pratly spoke, in an iron tone, he faced away from the cot, toward the sheriff. "Is this one of them?"

"Yes," Mike answered.

The older man's eyes were steadily direct and all-seeing. "We heard you killed one and brought another one back dyin'. Is this him?"

"Yes."

"Where's the dead one?"

"In boothill by now," Mike replied. "That's my brother's department, not mine."

"We also heard there was four of 'em. Where's the other two?"

"Why do you want to know?" Mike asked.

George Pratly turned and spoke. "Because we're goin' to hang 'em, Sheriff—that's why."

Mike shook his head, grey-level eyes on George Pratly's face. "Not while I'm alive, you're not."

The Pratlys looked at Locke Hibbard, who was standing near the table where the shotgun lay. As though taking a cue, Hibbard said: "Sheriff: we respect the law. We got no fight with you—but we're goin' to hang them killers today."

"Killers," Mike said sharply. "Yeah, they're killers, Locke—just like you're a killer. The difference is, they called out to Jack Arbuckle before they jumped the house. That's more'n you did to their friend Shiloh Smith."

The Pratlys were gazing at Hibbard, whose face flushed dark and whose voice grew hard in reply. "Who says I killed their friend?"

"Jack Arbuckle told his folks that before he was killed." Mike's look was saturnine. "Go ahead; deny it. Jack's dead."

"It's a damned lie."

"Is it?" Sheriff Mike said, turning toward the Pratlys.

"Did either of you talk to Mrs. Arbuckle before you came in town today?"

Jess did not speak, but his brother did: "No; we just come in," he said. "The womenfolk went over to Arbuckle's to fix up the dead."

Before Mike could speak the elder Pratly spoke: "It makes no difference, Shurf," he said in a gravelly tone. "If Locke killed that 'ere gunslinger he done a good thing. But them other gunslingers had no call to kill Jack and his paw—and we want 'em for that."

"You're dead right," Mike shot back at the older man. "They had no business attacking the Arbuckle place—although they thought Jack had killed their friend. If Locke, here, had had any guts, he'd have fought their friend out in plain sight, and none of the rest of this would have happened. As for me handing the other outlaws over to you—no. That's my answer, and it won't change."

Jess Pratly squinted at the sheriff, and when the others did not speak, he said: "Listen, Shurf; you can't stop us." A granite chin jutted toward the door. "There's a passel of us and there's one of you—an' if you think the folks hereabouts'll help you—guess again. The town-folk won't and neither will the cowmen. Now you just hand them fellers over."

Locke Hibbard was backing away from the table. A rumbling voice spoke from behind him. "Hold it, Hibbard!" Locke stopped and twisted to see Hugh Grant getting to his feet, a black scowl on his face. "You get cute in here an' I'll crush every bone in your carcass."

Silence settled again; the men glared at one another. Beyond the door restless feet moved on the plankwalk.

Finally the sheriff said: "Hibbard; you're under arrest for murder."

The cowboy's nostrils flared, otherwise he did not move. Sheriff Mike took up the shotgun and swung its snout to bear. "Hugh; disarm him."

The Pratlys surged forward. Grant stopped them with Hibbard's pistol. Behind the gun he looked huge and deadly. Mike motioned Velarde forward with the shotgun barrel.

"Lock him up."

George Pratly's face was crimson. "Sheriff; you're makin' a bad mistake. We come in here peaceable-like to talk. We could of come shootin'."

"Well," the sheriff replied dryly, swinging the shotgun a little. "It's not too late, if you're a mind to fight, George."

Velarde's big-rowelled spurs made the only sound; George Pratly let his pent up breath out slowly. "You're askin' for real trouble, Sheriff," he said icily.

Mike stood a moment longer holding the shotgun, then he placed it back on the table. Without Hibbard there would be no fight; he could relax. Watching Deputy Velarde return from locking Hibbard in a cell, the sheriff spoke to the Pratlys.

"All right, boys; you saw what happened to your crack gunfighter. Now visit the *Casino* if you have to, then mount up and hightail it for home."

George Pratly looked incredulous. "'You think you're goin' to get off that easy, McMahon?" he demanded.

Mike's answer was slow coming. "George," he said. "Let's understand one another. I run this town and this county. I don't scare easy and I don't give up prisoners. I *do* run drunks and troublemakers out of town, and sometimes I lock 'em up—and I don't need ten men at my back when I do it. Now you and Jess here know me, and you know I don't bluff. So you'd better walk soft." Mike jerked his head toward the door. "Now get out, and when I make my rounds an hour or so from now, I don't want to see you in town—because if I do, George, I'm going to lock you up, too."

Old Jess Pratly stumped furiously to the door and lifted the *tranca*. "You ain't goin' to live long enough to lock anybody up, Shurf. You got my damned word for that." He yanked the door open and passed from sight.

George Pratly also left the office, and his spurs had no sooner cleared the sill than Deputy Velarde slammed the door and lowered the bar.

Hugh Grant's troubled eyes came back around slowly. They rested on Mike McMahon's face while Grant shook his head. "You done that all wrong," he said flatly. "You should've locked the Pratlys up too."

"On what charge?"

"Charge!" Grant exploded. "Why, dammit Mike—any charge from horse stealin' to inciting a rebellion; at one time or another both those old devils've done one or the other—or both at the same time, and you know it as well as I do."

Mike sat down and pushed back his hat. "Not today they haven't," he said. "But maybe after nightfall they'll do both." He swivelled his head around. "Tom; you handled yourself right well. Now go out the back way and through the alley to the liverybarn. Tell Mr. Ward I want to see him at the back door. Tell Fred Nolan I want him, too." Mike looked steadily at the deputy. "You understand?"

"*Si;* in the alley, so I will not be seen."

Mike nodded and fished for his tobacco sack. Hugh Grant watched his hands for tremour; there was none. Grant got up and paced the room. "Now what?" he said.

The sheriff lit up and exhaled, and he could smile. It was a long, sound smile that showed the whiteness of his teeth. "Now they'll go to the *Casino* and take on a load of Dutch courage. That'll hold them until nightfall. After that they'll play their hand."

"Kill you, you mean, and take those lice out and hang 'em."

The sheriff said, "That's been tried before, Hugh, and I suppose someday someone'll do it, if I wear this badge long enough, but I know the men with the Pratlys; unless they get me like they got Smith, I don't think they can do it."

Grant stopped pacing and whirled around. "Ten-to-one? Why Mike—"

"Not ten-to-one, Hugh; you know folks wouldn't stand for that kind of a fight even if they do want to see Slidell's gang lynched. Face-to-face."

Grant went to the door and bent his head to listen. He heard nothing and straightened up. "It's too quiet out there. I don't like it."

Mike got up, crossed to the door and opened it. "Go on, Hugh," he said. "Get some fresh air. Your nerves are showing."

Grant hesitated, then he passed along as far as the plankwalk. "I'll get something, but it won't be fresh air," he retorted, and strode purposefully north through the heat-waves, the solitary pedestrian on the west side of Front Street.

Mike gazed along the road. There were dozens of horses lounging at the hitchrails, and along the west walk where the sun hadn't yet reached, a few men loafed in the shade, saying little, standing easy, waiting.

At the *Casino's* sturdy tie-rack horses were jammed close. Even from that distance Mike could make out familiar hip brands. A top-buggy whirred along and cut in close before Doctor Pat's office. A woman got down heavily and helped a young boy to alight; he had one arm wrapped in a blanket and his sweat-shiny face was grey. The woman hustled the boy into the office and closed the door. Fell out of an apple tree, Mike thought, or was sneaking a ride on the colts in the pasture and one jumped him off and broke his arm.

He shifted his stance slightly so that he could command a good view of the *Casino's* doorway. Men came and went occasionally, but none were the men from Skull Valley. A hard, sharp rap on the back door recalled him into the office. After barring the front entrance he went out past the cells and lifted the bar on a heavily reinforced rear door. It groaned when he swung it back. Deputy Velarde pushed quickly inside followed by Ed Ward and Fred Nolan. The liveryman's face was ashen. Mike sent Tom for the keys on his desk, and by the time Velarde had returned Mike had explained his plan to the saddlemaker and the liveryman. Later, when the sheriff and his deputy returned to the office, the injured man by the stove was calling for water. They gave it to him. When he finished drinking he threw a long, appraising glance at the sheriff.

"You sure told them old gaffers off," he said.

"Well, you can bet your last dollar they won't stay told off, Sheridan," the sheriff replied. "And I wouldn't bet they wouldn't try to hang you, wound or no wound."

"You're not going to let 'em, are you?"

"No; but there's quite a crew of them."

Sheridan forced himself up on one elbow and his face was flushed from the effort and the pain. "Listen, Sheriff; like that big feller said, you could sneak us out of here."

Mike sat on the edge of the table regarding Sheridan. "Why should I? What're you to me?"

Sheridan looked more surprised than frightened. "Whoa up there," he said. "You told them old gaffers you wouldn't surrender a prisoner to 'em, any time."

"Correct; but I didn't say I was going to get killed over you and your friends, either."

The wounded man stared hard. "You mean, if they come after us with guns, you'll let them have us?"

"I said I wouldn't get killed over you. Interpret it any way you want to."

Sheridan swore and sank back down. "You're a hell of a sheriff," he said bitterly.

"There's nothing original about that," Mike answered crossing to the side of the cot. "Tell me something, Sheridan; how many places have a reward on your head?"

The outlaw's eyes went to Mike's face, and his expression changed gradually. In a soft voice he said. "I get it. You'll trade a little. Well; you hide me and I'll tell you some stories."

"You'll tell me first. Where are you wanted?"

"I'm not wanted, but Curt and Dominguez are—that's all

147

I'll tell you, now."

Mike stood in thought for a moment, then he went to the table, scribbled a note, gave it to Deputy Velarde with instructions to deliver it to Epifanio Chavez, and as soon as Velarde left, he sat down near the cot.

"All right, Sheridan; you'll be taken out of here after dark. Now—tell me the stories."

Matthew Sheridan talked; Slidell and Belasco were both wanted in Texas. Mike listened and, as the afternoon wore on, outside the jailhouse Vacaville's lethargy dissipated gradually, and when Tom Velarde returned he informed the sheriff of two things; one, 'Pifas had agreed to do as the sheriff asked, after dark, and, although it was still broad daylight, Vacaville's storekeepers were putting up their shutters, and some were even closing their shops and leaving the area of Front Street.

Sheridan watched Mike go to the gun-rack and take down a shotgun, sling it under his arm and cross to the door. Beads of sweat stood out upon the outlaw's face. "Hey," he called. "Suppose them fellers don't wait to jump the jailhouse until after dark?"

Mike did not answer. He told Tom to keep a sharp watch, and that he would be back after making his rounds. When the deputy and the renegade were alone, the latter swore with impotent, frightened anger, until Velarde shut him up.

Outside, where evening coolness was sweeping in low from the shadowed mountains, Mike stood still looking down the run of empty roadway, then he began walking, staying to the east side of Front Street. Near Hatfield's Cafe he came unexpectedly upon Antonia. She stopped for a long look into his face and put a hand on his arm.

"You shouldn't be uptown this evening," he said. "Better get along home, Toni."

"Yes—I know." Her hand dropped away and the sweep of lashes went to the shotgun. "Mike . . ."

He pulled himself straight before her, seeing the way her lips lay soft, pliably soft, then when she returned her eyes to his face, he saw the waiting silence there; the smoky-eyed expectancy. He spoke: "You'd better go along now."

"Yes."

He moved past and she listened to the hard fall of his bootsteps, then turned and watched the thickness of his back move down through the shadows. Finally, she started south toward the Grant Street cross-way, and when she looked around for the last time, he was nearing the livery-barn, where she had just come from.

G.B. Buckholz was standing just inside the door of the barn. He didn't see the sheriff until Mike was suddenly there in the strong-scented gloom. G.B. gave a start, his hand tightened around a carbine he was holding, then he made a rueful smile.

"Hell," the hostler said with loud relief, "you like to snuck up on me, Mike."

An easy glance went to the gun in Buckholz's hand and stayed there a moment. "Expecting Indians, G.B.?"

"Uh—well—mebbe. Mebbe not." Buckholz changed the subject. "Uh—that Ward feller's a right nice *hombre*." The hostler's grin became flat and forced. "He likes beer, too; and say, he's a pretty good liveryman."

"Had experience, has he?"

"Oh pshaw," G.B. said quickly. "He's an old hand. Y'know, a feller works around stock most of his life, he can tell another feller who has, too, in mighty short order."

Mike's slow smile started up. "I reckon so," he said, and started to move on. "Well; you boys be careful where you step—the weather's warming up again."

G.B. watched him pass on down the walk for a moment then resumed his vigil. Across the road men's voices came loudly from the *Casino*. Next to the saloon, two slouching Mexicans were seated on the bench in front of a general store, asleep or nearly so. Southerly, near John Hunt's law office, Hugh Grant and the lawyer stood back in the shadows in conversation. Even from that distance, G.B. could tell from the way the big man was standing, that he was not relaxed.

Mike crossed the road where the plankwalk ran out, then started south. He stopped in the doorway of Fred Nolan's shop and spoke briefly to someone inside, then came as far as Charley Householder's saloon. There, Will Herman, who had been watching his progress over the spindle-doors, leaned something against the inner wall and walked out with a false grin. Will's face was pale and sweaty.

"Fine evening," he said, and Mike's eyes twinkled at him.

"Sure is. Like the Indians say—this is a good day to die."

Herman's breath rattled. "That's not very damned funny," he snapped. "They're getting drunk in there, Mike."

"Yeh; I know. Must take a lot of whiskey. They been there a couple of hours."

"Are you going in?"

The sheriff shook his head, looking toward the *Casino*. "No; I'm just making my evenin' round."

Will's gaze followed along the walk as far as the *Casino*. His mind was full but his lips were locked flat. He said nothing, and after a moment the sheriff walked on. Will ducked back into the saloon and swore under his breath because the swift-falling desert night was thickening, pressing in under the overhang and hindering his view.

In front of the general store, next to *Carleton's Casino*, Mike slowed to peer at two loose-sitting Mexicans on a bench. Without lifting his head, one said: "*Jefe;* the injured man is hidden."

Mike stopped, brows lowering. " 'Pifas; what are you doing here?"

Thin shoulders rose and fell. Chavez opened his serape for a second and two tied-down guns shone stark and dull in the murky light. "Time was," he said in Spanish, "when I too, made the long day's journey into night, friend." The dark face lifted, a bland smile showed. "My friend and I . . ." Another shrug. "Just once more—for old time's sake—before we become old men—my friend and I think it would be a grand thing to smell smoke."

Mike looked at the other Mexican, but his hat hid his face; he neither looked up nor spoke. "I appreciate what you're meaning to do," he said to Chavez. "But don't do it. I don't want any shooting if it can be helped."

"But of a certainty, *jefe*. Old men don't start fights."

"Why don't you go watch over the wounded man for me?"

"He has more guards now, than he needs," Chavez replied, showing in his face that he had no intention of moving.

The sheriff sighed, said: "*Hijo 'mano,*" and started forward, and as soon as his attention was removed from Chavez and his companion, it came swiftly to him that the discordant sound of voices was no longer coming from *Carleton's Casino*. A deep and deliberate silence lay behind the saloon's doors. He shifted the scatter-gun, snugged it up under his left arm, and walked on, footfalls sounding thunder-loud in the purpling, warm silence. He came even with the doors and slowed but did not stop. Beyond, another fifty feet, John Hunt and Hugh Grant were like stone, watching.

"Hey, Sheriff . . ."

Mike came slowly around, feeling the run of tightness going along his muscles. He recognised the voice.

Carl Braun stood there just outside the *Casino*, dark, Indian-face watching the sheriff with close attentiveness, long, thin mouth pulled straight. "You never give Locke a chance, Sheriff, throwin' down on him like that."

"What do you know about it—you weren't there."

"I heard; we all heard how it was—you and the greaser deputy and the big fat feller . . ."

"You're drunk," Mike said quietly, contempt more than anger in his words.

"Not too drunk, Sheriff. Come on; walk out into the road with me."

Braun was moving when a sharp snippet of sound froze him. He had not seen the hand move, but the shotgun was cocked now, its ugly snout less than fifteen feet from his middle. He kept looking down like a man in a trance.

"You'd better go stay with Hibbard until you sober up, Carl. I don't want to have to kill you."

Braun's eyes lifted, dark, muddy eyes with fire-points

lying in them. "Not just yet," he said. "Let's just sort of figure this out, Sheriff."

Mike acted as though he hadn't heard. "Use your left hand—unbuckle that shell-belt and let it drop."

Braun remained motionless; after a long interval he smiled, a cold, dangerous death's-head smile. "You got a surprise comin', Sheriff."

"*Drop that gun-belt!*"

Braun made no move to comply. He held his smile, and the dangerous look in his eyes. Then his face blanked, his head half-turned, and his breath ran out. A spidery dark hand had reached from behind, removed his belt-gun and tossed it out into the dark dust of the roadway. Braun did not actually see the Mexican behind him; he heard just the barest slither of leather over boards, and caught a soft blur of movement. He swore and faced forward again.

"Couldn't do it alone, could you?" he said to Sheriff Mike. "Well; that's all right. If I don't get you Locke will— or one of the others."

"For the last time, Carl—*drop that belt!*"

Braun fumbled at the buckle and the sound of leather striking wood came; a whisper of sound in the stillness. Sheriff Mike gestured with the shotgun: "Now walk."

He marched Braun across the empty road to the jailhouse and waited beyond the door until Tom Velarde came back, key-ring in one hand, short-gun in the other hand. "He is locked up, *jefe,*" Velarde said, darting a sharp glance toward the *Casino.* "There are others . . ." His voice trailed off. "Four of them."

Mike shook his head. "Those other two, apart a ways, aren't Skull Valleyers. One's Hugh Grant, the other's

John Hunt."

Darkness lay just beyond vision, fringing Front Street with its opaqueness, its velvet-soft stillness. The men in the shadows of *Carleton's Casino* were a blur. Mike wished for daylight. Velarde looked from the motionless men to the sheriff and back again. From the lawyer's office two lamps came quickeningly to life. Someone had placed them side by side in the window so that they cast a permeating yellowness outward and along the plankwalk. The deputy sighed.

"That is better," he said.

Other lights appeared; at the liverybarn two large carriage lamps, one on either side of the doorway, glowed with strong, white light. Front Street, between Nolan's saddlery and Hatfield's Cafe, showed pale and distinct. Mike had never seen it so well lighted. In his brother's office light shone brightly, washing over a dark-coated figure standing to one side of the doorway leaning on something that glistened metallically.

Velarde's eyes moved slowly along the roadway; his words came softly. "There are men on both sides of the road, *jefe*."

Mike shifted the shotgun to his right hand. "Yeah."

"Those Pratlys have placed their men well."

"No," the sheriff said slowly, "those aren't the Skull Valley men. Take another look at them. I don't know who figured this out—probably Hugh Grant but those are local fellers."

"*Ai*," the deputy said softly, comprehension flooding into his face. "*Seguro*. That one far down is G.B. The fat one there—that is *Señor* Hatfield. Over there is Nolan—there, the bartender . . ."

A cold smile touched Sheriff Mike's lips. "Yeah; maybe we've got a few friends after all. See those two sitting on the bench by the general store? One's 'Pifas and the other one's a dark-faced man with a big gold ring on his right hand. I didn't see his face."

Velarde's eyes swept to the silhouettes. He said: "It is too bad you didn't see his face, *jefe;* it is not a pretty face—it is badly pock-marked."

"Oh? You know the man?"

"*Si;* but it as well that you don't."

Mike said no more. He drew up, let the hammers of the shotgun down, and jerked his head at Velardc. The deputy moved farther back into the office but he did not at once close and bar the door.

The sheriff was in the middle of the road when a voice called out to him; a curt, hard voice he recognised even though it was now thicker than before. "McMahon!"

He kept walking, but changed course so that he would halt before the *Casino* where the Pratlys stood side by side. When he was close he answered: "Yes."

"You think you got things runnin' your way, don't you?" George Pratly said.

"I'm keeping order, George. If you want to start something—go ahead."

The older Pratly's face was fish-belly colour in the reflected light; his expression was stony. "We got two scores to settle with you, now, Shurf. You can save some grief by lettin' our boys go."

Mike looked long into Jess Pratly's face before he replied. "I'll let them go, when you pass me your word the lot of you'll hit the trail and stay out of town for ten days."

Jess Pratly's thin body was ramrod straight. He made a flat laugh, short and spiked-sounding. "We'll leave directly, Shurf. Won't be long now." An interval of silence ensued, then Jess Pratly spoke again: "You're goin' to see that you ain't so high an' mighty, Shurf. You'll find out . . ."

Something stirred uneasily in Mike's mind. He searched the lined face in front of him, then George Pratly was speaking again.

"We see them fellers you got placed around, Sheriff. They won't help you much, though."

"I didn't place them. They're men who believe as I do—that the law will take care of Arbuckle's killers."

"We got law, too. Pretty damned good law."

"Lynch- and gun-law, George. That was all right when there wasn't any other kind—but now there is." Mike paused, hearing the great silence. "Listen, George; you fellers haven't done anything yet—there's still time for you to come to your senses. The Arbuckle killers will be tried for murder in another week or so. There are witnesses against them. There's even a confession from the one we shot. They'll get the rope for what they did. Don't get yourselves in trouble by trying to do what the law will do anyway."

"In Skull Valley," Jesse Pratly interrupted to say, "we been fightin' our own battles for a mighty long time, Shurf, and we done just fine at it. We ain't goin' to change now, just because some lop-eared judge thinks he can do better."

The faint showing of hope died in Mike's gaze, and his expression hardened. "All right. You've called the play. Go

156

ahead; start something."

"Ain't quite the time yet," Jess said. "Got a few minutes yet to wait."

Mike frowned. "What do you mean by that?"

The elder Pratly said no more. His brother, George, raised his head looking south where the light ran out and shadows lay dark. He had heard a door being wrenched open. It was a loud sound in the hush. When he spoke he was looking across the road and down a ways, and his voice was strong with triumph.

"There, McMahon; turn around and take a good look."

Mike moved only his head at first, but then his entire body came around. Scuffling past the door of his office were a number of shapes. One, sagging heavy between two others, was scoring the roadway dust with dragging toes. He recognised that one at first sight; Deputy Velarde. It took only a moment to guess what had happened. The Skull Valley men had slipped through dark alleys and come up behind the jailhouse. Somehow, they had badgered Velarde into opening the door for them. They had then struck him down and released both Locke Hibbard and Carl Braun.

Velarde's body was permitted to sink against the earth. The other men began to fan out across the road. In the middle of their uneven line a short, compact silhouette spread its legs and Carl Braun's voice called out:

"Sheriff; ain't no sneakin' greaser behind me now."

The taller blur beside Braun, recognisable by the soft light of a slowly rising moon off silver conchos, was Locke Hibbard. Without being able to see them, Mike knew Hibbard's eyes were hot with anticipation, his chest was rising and falling quickly with exhilaration. Then Hibbard said: "All right, McMahon—you asked for it—gettin' the drop on me. I get first crack at you. Let's see if I'm a bushwhacker or not. This is a stand-up shoot-out." Hibbard paused. "Better shuck that scatter-gun—it won't reach this far."

Mike was like stone. Off on his left there was a slow sound of movement. He longed to look around, to see if it was the Pratlys, but he did not.

"Big odds," he called to Hibbard. "Ten-to-one."

"No; this is just between you and me. If you down me, then Carl gets a whack at you. Them other boys're just makin' sure it goes off fair-like."

Mike said: "I wish I could talk you out of this, Locke. It's not going to be just you and me—or Carl and me. It's going to be Vacaville against Skull Valley, and whichever way it ends, it's going to cause bad blood for a long time come."

Two voices spoke at once. Locke Hibbard said: "I think you're turnin' coyote, Sheriff," and Jess Pratly's hard words dropped like iron: "Shoot or get shot, Shurf—fish or cut bait. You asked for it—*now damn you take it!*"

CHAPTER TEN

CARL BRAUN'S VOICE arose into the electric stillness, addressed to the Pratlys. "Them other fellers aren't in there," Braun said. "He must've sent 'em to Junction City."

George Pratly was looking hard at the sheriff. "Hold on a minute, Locke," he called, then lowered his voice. "What'd you do with the other two killers, Sheriff?"

"I arrested them."

"Yeah; we know that. Where are they now—in the Junction City jail?"

"There's a good way for you to find out," Mike answered, watching Locke Hibbard.

For a moment the Pratlys spoke in low tones together, then the older man edged forward to the lip of the walkway. "You got one minute to tell us, Shurf. If you don't we'll hunt 'em up—but you won't be around to see it."

Mike ignored the older man. When he spoke he looked straight at the dark blur of Locke Hibbard. "Go on, Locke—you want to fight—*Draw!*"

The last word ripped out. Hibbard went low and forward. His gun was half free of the holster when Sheriff Mike's first bullet drove him back. The gun was dangling from numbing fingers when the second shot broke Hibbard in the middle. He went down slowly into the dust and didn't move.

"*You—Carl!*" The sheriff said, and his gunbarrel swung a fraction. Braun had begun to draw his weapon before Locke Hibbard fell. He completed the draw, was thumbing back the dog when the bullet caught him squarely in the forehead. His weapon exploded, the bullet furrowing into the ground ten feet ahead of where his body came to rest.

Someone fired from the edge of the plankwalk. Mike saw nothing but the quick-bursting flash of flame, then he was down and rolling in the dust, and above him gunfire broke out in a deafening volley. Dust from the roadway jerked to life where the sheriff had been. He got to the plankwalk and twisted to see where the Pratlys were. One,

George Pratly, was stumbling backwards doubled over. Less than ten feet from him stood Epifanio Chavez and his friend; both were firing with each hand, and as Mike watched, Jess Pratly's legs folded and he fell with a limp sound.

Men who, seconds before, had edged out of *Carleton's Casino* to see a gunfight, were now fighting their way back inside. Sounds arose over the gunfire; curses and yells. Carleton's hitchrail went down with a crash and six frenzied horses went careening through the dusk trailing broken reins.

From the liverybarn two rifles were in action. Each time one boomed, a voice would ring out with a happy curse. Mike heard the solid sound of bullets striking wood and got to his knees, crouching there seeking a target. Behind him Epifanio Chavez called out in Spanish, telling him to lie flat.

From the south end of town six Skull Valley gunmen poured a fierce fire northward. There was nothing to see of them but gun-flashes, and although the return-fire was equally savage, it became obvious, since the six guns continued to fire, that their owners moved each time they shot.

Mike scuttled past the two Mexicans, who were holding themselves flat against the front of a store, and zig-zagged to a narrow opening between two buildings. He disappeared into the darkness there. 'Pifas Chavez, who had seen, elbowed his companion and they both ran after the sheriff.

Where Mike emerged into the alleyway behind the *Casino*, moonlight winked off broken bottles and a conglomeration of trash. He stayed as close to the black backs of buildings as he could, moving south. Then, where a thrust of siding jutted outward, he halted, listening. Around front the fight was continuing unabated. Where the sheriff stood, the sound was loud. He began edging around the building, was nearly clear of it when he encountered a green window. A square glint of light shone outward; it would limn him perfectly, so he stopped again. He could not see beyond the light and the sickly path it made at his feet, and for a while he was motionless, then he sprang forward and landed on the far side; his feet kicked a rattle of cans. Nearby, with darkness dripping on him, a man pulled up sharply and whirled around. Mike had only a glimpse of him, and of the gun in his fist; he dropped down in the formless substance of night. A red stab of flame whipped over his head and shoulders. He tilted his own weapon and tugged it—the pistol was empty. He threw it, saw the shapeless man wince, then he hurtled himself forward low and fast, twisting to throw a blow and dodge away from the swinging gun-arm at the same time. The shot rang with a hurting echo inside the sheriff's head, and he smelt the powder from it.

His fist caught the unseen face and held it far back for a brief moment, then he reached wildly with both hands for the gun, got the arm, twisted it back with a savage lunge of his entire weight, and the gun dropped as gristle ground against bone. The stranger was whip-sawing his breath with agony. Mike released the arm and moved to throw another blow. At that moment the shadow grunted, its knee came up and caught the sheriff in the belly. He bent low, air belching out past his lips. A bony fist grazed the skin of his jaw leaving a red welt, then he was weaving away and the stranger missed a two-handed blow, nearly lost his balance and was recovering when Mike closed in, grabbed the man and locked him in a straining grip.

They staggered out of the green light into pure darkness, their feet grinding through cans, broken glass, and refuse, to the flinty earth below. Mike freed one hand and sledged a short blow upwards. A flash of hot pain raced along his upper arm and for a second the body straining with him, grew sodden. But only for the second, then the stranger was arching and whipping and straining to break free, his panting breath rasping out in bursts.

Where twin wagon ruts scored deep into the alley, the bodies crashed down. Dust flew up around them. Mike felt hot pain when the man under him kicked upwards and caught him on the leg. He saw a blur of movement rising and dodged aside. The fist caught him above the ear, jarring him without pain, then the stranger was throwing him off and straining to his feet. He got free and turned to aim a wild kick. Mike ducked under it, grabbed at the man's leg, caught only the whiplash of his trousers, then the man was fleeing. Mike raced after him, caught hold of his shell-belt with one hand from behind, and hung on. The stranger wrenched around and tore free. He staggered, then, and Mike got hold with both hands. Behind them was a high board fence. Scarcely conscious of doing it, the sheriff caught the stranger around the middle, lifted him bodily, and flung him outwards. The fence shook and a loud cracking sound came from behind the stranger's head. His knees folded. He almost went down. Mike grabbed him, lifted him with straining arms, and threw him back again. That time the man bounced off the fence and fell into

Mike's arms, hands scrabbling feebly. Mike pushed him off and swung a free-hand blow; his fist sank to the wrist in the stranger's belly and he turned soft and slack.

Mike gulped for the warm night air and his body hurt in a half a dozen places. He bent, caught the unconscious man by the yoke of his shirt and began dragging him along the alley. Two shadows rose up out of darkness. He let go of his prisoner and crouched. Epifanio Chavez's voice came to him in a low purr.

"*Perfecto, jefe.* A good fight."

Mike straightened slowly, stiffly. He ran a torn sleeve across his mouth where a split lip trickled blood. "I'm glad it's you, 'Pifas. I threw my gun at him."

Chavez's companion held out a long-barrelled Colt, butt first. In the weak light his broad, dark face was split into a smile and the white surfaces of teeth shone. He spoke rapidly in Spanish. Epifanio said: "He knows no English *jefe.* What he says is 'a brave man deserves the best weapon'."

Mike squinted and bobbed his head. "*Gracias, compadre. Muchas gracias.*"

The man moved closer. Small, black eyes set in a ravished, pock-marked face, shown warmly. "*Por nada,*" he said in a pleasant voice, then looked down and spoke again to Chavez, who shrugged.

"Who is he, *jefe?*"

Mike bent, rolled the stranger over and peered into his face. "Slick Bennett—one of the Skull Valley men." Mike grasped the shirt again and started forward. The Mexicans each took one of Bennett's arms. In that way they dragged him to the rear of *Carleton's Casino* where Mike meant to leave him, but, finding the rear door locked, they dragged Bennett farther along the alley, until they came to the rear of Nolan's saddle shop. There, after much pounding, Mike got Fred to open the door a slit. "Here," he said, pushing Bennett inside. "That's another one for you to watch."

They were moving toward the opening between two buildings when a bullet splintered wood above them. All three men fell quickly into the shadows, then a voice Mike recognised as belonging to his brother, shouted: "Three of them up here—come on—be quick."

The pock-marked Mexican was swinging his gun to bear when Mike caught his arm and forced it down, then he sang out. "Pat—you idiot—it's me—Mike."

"Sure," a shrill voice called back. "An' I'm Ulysses S. Grant, too. Stand up—all three of you—and keep your damned hands high—real high."

Epifanio made a sibilant whisper. "Stay down, *jefe*. Let them show first."

The sheriff called: "Who's with you, Pat?"

"Hugh, John Hunt, Amos. Who's that lying there with you?"

The sheriff got slowly to his feet, staring southward. "All right; here I am," he said. "Come on over." Doctor Pat said something indistinguishable, to the men with him, then they all came trooping through the refuse of the alley, guns naked and loosely held. The two Mexicans got up facing forward. The pockmarked man looked anxiously at Chavez, finally a ripple of Spanish passed his lips and Chavez replied; it was all right; he recognised the *gringos*.

Pat stopped, put his carbine against the ground and leaned on it. "You look like you've been through the meat grinder at Hausehofer's store." he said to the sheriff.

"I've seen neater looking physicians, in my time," his brother replied.

Beyond Pat were his companions. Mike regarded them briefly, then started forward. "Come on; with this many men we can get behind them."

"Hold it," the doctor said, twisting to follow his brother's progress. "Are you deaf?"

Mike stopped in his tracks. The night was still and echoless.

"It's over," Pat said.

They moved down through the stygian darkness between the buildings and came out on Front Street. A man's voice rose high to call out a name. Other men moved through the yellow light toward dark things lying upon the ground.

Mike went directly to where he had last seen Tomas Velarde. The deputy was not there. A small group of men over by the *Casino* saw him in the roadway and one called to him. Trailed by Doctor Pat and Hugh Grant, the two Mexicans and a bartender, Mike crossed to where solicitous hands were pouring whiskey into—and over—Deputy Velarde. Mike reached out. "Are you hurt, Tom?"

Velarde smiled a quick flash of teeth. "No, *jefe,* they only hit me on the head—but this is good whiskey and it costs me nothing."

A fat hand fell across Mike's arm. He turned. It was Amos Hatfield. "Sheriff; Nolan says to come get your prisoners; he dassn't leave the shop, and he's missing all the fun."

Mike looked around. "Are you up to it, Tom?"

"*Si.* This was nothing."

"Then take 'em back and lock 'em up."

As the deputy walked away, taking Chavez and the pock-marked man with him, Doctor Pat was elbowed aside by Hugh Grant, who was wearing a faint expression of perplexity. "Is what I'm thinkin' correct, Mike?"

"Well now, Hugh, I'm not a—"

"Who's Nolan holding prisoner down at the saddle shop?"

"Slick Bennett for one," the sheriff replied. "He and I had a little tussle out in the alley. He's also holding Curt Slidell."

"What!"

"Dammit, Hugh; you kept telling me the Skull Valleyers, would break into the jail—that I couldn't hold my prisoners." The sheriff felt in a torn shirt pocket for his tobacco sack. It wasn't there. Doctor Pat offered his, and the sheriff began making a cigarette. "Fred Nolan took Slidell out of the jailhouse the back way, up to his place, hung an apron on him and set him there at the work-table, and sat behind the curtain to his living quarters with a gun on Slidell."

"What about the other one—Belasco?"

"Ed Ward, the new manager at the liverybarn, took him over. He put him to dunging out stalls under a gun." At Grant's incredulous expression, Mike grinned. "Well; I couldn't have gotten them to Junction City—and even if I had, the Skull Valleyers would have gotten them anyway, so I just sort of put them both out in plain sight—the only person who wasn't in plain sight, was the man who watched them for me with a cocked gun in his hand."

"Yeah—well—"

"Epifanio Chavez and some friends of his took Matt

Sheridan down to Old Town and put him to bed there."

Grant scowled and scratched his belly. "That plumb puzzled me," he said, "when Hibbard and them others came out of the jailhouse dragging your deputy by himself. I was still tryin' to make sense out of what Braun called to George Pratly, when the battle started."

Pat left the crowd when a woman's light voice spoke his name. He followed Eliza Ward into his office and closed the door. As he was shedding his coat, Mrs. Ward pointed toward the leather sofa. A man lay there, bare from the waist up, naked breast a startling white contrast to the dark tan of his glistening face. There was a purple swelling near the collarbone and a deep red slash under his ribs. Doctor Pat crossed the room and looked down, then he spoke in a blunt tone: "You damned old fool you; what d'you mean, getting tangled up in a ruckus like this?"

Two squinty old eyes glared upwards and Stone Gorman said: "I ain't going to take your lip, too, so get to digging and patching." As Pat bent a probing finger, Gorman closed his eyes, pinched them closed. "Four dead out there," he said through lips that scarcely moved. "Jess an' George—Carl and Locke. We come to town to hang four— not lose four."

"Eliza," Pat said. "Clean him up first—I swear this old devil hasn't had a bath since the year one."

Stone raised a long, scrawny arm to ward off Eliza's approach. "No," he keened. "No woman's going to give me no bath."

Doctor Pat bent from the waist and waggled a long finger. "You shut up and lie still or I'll get some of the boys in here to hold you down." He straightened up. "Go ahead, Eliza."

Gorman's dark, leathery face burned a slow crimson and he gritted his teeth as though Doctor Pat was digging the bullet from his shoulder. His lips were so tightly locked that when the doctor asked him a question he had difficulty answering.

"Stone: why did you do it? Why did you listen to the others? You're not a young man, so you should've known better."

Gorman opened his eyes to a slit. He fixed a rigid stare on the doctor and when Eliza Ward came into his focus he stared through her. "I was thinkin' the same thing when I was lyin' out there in the dust and dark. I—guess it was because them whelps widowed Elizabeth."

"Yeh; Miz' Arbuckle. You see; thirty years ago we was pretty close—then along come Jack's paw and she married him."

"Oh," Doctor Pat said softly, and moved toward the centre of the room as the door swung inward and Sheriff Mike entered, stood still a moment gazing at Stone Gorman, then faced the doctor.

"I've cleaned out the Pratlys, Carl Braun and Locke Hibbard, Pat; you can plant them any time you're ready."

"Yes; in the morning. Let me look at that bruise on your—"

"No; it'll be all right." The grey-level eyes went back to the couch. "Him too?" Mike asked.

"Yes; only small wounds though."

"Well," Mike said, fingering his ruined, filthy shirt. "I've got some chores to do." He started out through the doorway.

"Mike?"

"Yes?" The sheriff turned back.

"Have you locked Slidell and Belasco up again?"

"Sure; twenty minutes ago."

"And had the bodies put in the shed?"

"Say," the sheriff said in protest. "Why don't you just come out and say it—whatever it is?"

"Well all right—give her a kiss for me, too."

Mike closed the door, drew in a big breath, and started south. He crossed the road westerly at the Grant Street intersection, and continued on to his own house. There, he cleaned up, bathed his bruises, used caustic on the cracked lip, then went back out into the night.

Now the moon was full up, and a mist of stars all run together in the high purple added to the watery light. At the corner of Grant Street, he paused long enough to watch the bustle and activity; to observe men moving from group to group; to see riders coming and going; and to think for a short moment of the women in Skull Valley who were waiting to hear their men returning. Then he went to the jailhouse and sat down at his table looking straight ahead at the old adobe wall.

Later, when Deputy Velarde came in wearing his hat well forward so it wouldn't touch the swollen lump beneath, and balancing two trays of food, the sheriff said: "What about the wounded one?"

"*Señor* Chavez is having him taken to the doctor's office, *jefe*."

"And you—you want to go home and get some rest?"

Tom shrugged, still balancing the trays. "*No importado*," he said. "It is not important. I will wait."

"Wait? Wait for what?"

"Until you return." The dark eyes shone with a soft smile. "There are those who will want to know that you are unhurt."

Mike got up stiffly and moved toward the door. "I won't be long," he said, and passed out into the night.

"That will be a shame, then," Velarde said to himself, took up the keys and started for the cell-block.

The walk down Grant Street was peaceful. Mike had trouble blending recent events with the present solitude around him. At Antonia's gateway he paused a moment to finish a cigarette. His last inhalation agitated the little red tip and glowing smoulder lit up the lines at the outer corners of his eyes, then it fell to the ground and died under his heel.

"Mike . . ."

She was there on the porch in a chair, and the way she was hunched forward slightly, as though throwing her weight against dread and uncertainty, told him enough.

"Yes," he said, and went up the walk, up the sagging steps to the darkness beyond.

"I've been waiting." She touched the arm of a chair close by hers. "Sit down."

He did. He sat down and pushed his legs far out and let looseness settle over him. The night ran on to the far meeting of sky and earth, with a big wash of stars.

Somewhere, uptown, a group of horsemen clattered over the flinty earth; it would be riders in from one of the ranches. They would hear what had happened and be surprised.

Farther down Grant Street, near where it ended against

the desert, a woman called through the darkness, and a boy answered. A rig went past out in the road stirring a froth of dark dust to life. Antonia felt the peacefulness too, and did not break its solitude for a long time, then she said: "It was like a war, Mike . . ."

"A skirmish anyway," he replied, picking up her train of thought. "I guess you'll want to know; four of the Skull Valley men were killed."

Silence settled again, and except for the serenity it was the same; darkly quiet and endless.

"Because of me," she said finally.

He considered that, and undoubtedly it was true, but on the other hand he knew it would only have been a matter of time before someone would have shot it out with Porter Buel, and whether it was a hired gunman or not, the Skull Valley people would have sought vengeance. That was the way they were, and always had been. In a way, it was good the way it had come about, because if a townsman had killed Buel, the fight would have been between the ranchers and the villagers; it would have left a smouldering feud behind. This way, the antagonisms would not live beyond the present generation.

He stole a sidelong glance at her profile. A strange and solemn expression lay across her face. "Don't blame yourself entirely," he said. "There's nothing simple about living, and no sure answer for any of us. Punishment for a thing like this is in memory. I know; I've seen it before. In a lot of ways a memory's much worse than a hangrope."

"I know that, Mike. I know it already."

He reached for her hand, and held it. "There was some justification for you, Toni. You're not the first person who has killed for revenge, and you sure won't be the last. I reckon we were meant to be that way—all of us."

"If I could only have seen ahead."

"Not many of us have that gift," he said.

She swung to look straight at him. "But—you'll always think of that, when you think of me, Mike."

"No," he answered slowly. "If I was like that I'd be pretty busy remembering things about folks so's I could hate them. I'm built differently. Like I told you before; everyone makes mistakes. The only time I draw off from them a little, is when they make the same mistake over and over again." His hand closed tightly around her fingers, and he was still for so long she almost reached over to touch him, then he looked around at her, and even in the gloom she could see the strange look on his face; part sadness, part something very close to smiling. Quite suddenly he got up, drawing her up with him by the hand, and drew her close against him with his powerful arms. This, she thought, is like the first night; like every time they were close now, and yet there was a difference too, for this time hatred, death, and tragedy, lay out in the night somewhere, far out and receding; it was not a part of what she was doing.

She lifted her lips for the strong pressure of his mouth; a deeply satisfying feeling spread through her and she met his force with force of her own.

They stood like that, close and mingling in the dark night with a scent of dust in the hot air and stars hanging brilliantly high above, until she pushed back and looked up into his face, waiting. Then, when he did not say it, she did.

"I'm in love with you, Mike. I have been since that first night. It's such a different love from what I felt for Reed."

172

The strong pound of his heart was uneven and loud. He brushed his lips across her mouth and said: "I want to marry you, Toni, but that's nothing new. I've thought about you like that for a long time; only when Reed came along—well—it seemed more natural for him to have you than me. He was younger, and I guess he was smarter. I just quit hoping after that."

"You were always so distant, Mike. So sort of big and capable and, well, formidable. I've always thought of you as a handsome man—especially when I was still in school—but you were unobtainable; so distant . . ."

He drew his head back gazing down. The twinkle was in his eye. "Not very distant now," he said, and smiled into her eyes. "Will you marry me?"

"Yes. I want to marry you, Mike." She was silent briefly, then: "Mike? No regrets? No memories?"

"Well; you can never escape memories, Toni, but I promise you there will never be any regrets. Not for me, anyway."

"Or me."

"I expect you know there'll be days and nights when I'll be gone."

She moved out of the enclosure of his arms and stood near an upright looking out. "Yes. I thought of that this evening, while I was waiting. I thought how it must be for sheriffs' wives." She faced him, and dark shadows lay across her. "Like you said: there's no sure answer for any of us. I'll learn to cope with that, Mike. I'll learn to live with it—and to make a home for you that you'll come back to."

A smoky look was in his eyes. "When?" he asked.

"When will you marry me, Toni?"

It was her turn to smile. "Is tonight too late?" she said. "Right now? As soon as I get my shawl and walk uptown with you?"

His white teeth shown in a slow grin. "No," he said with slow gravity, "I don't think it's too late—not for me, although I'll give you five-to-one odds the preacher'll be abed."

She continued to look at him for an interval of silence, then she said: "Are you sure, Mike? Do you really want this?"

"I do."

"And—you won't think of Reed—or the other thing?"

"No."

"Then kiss me again."

He did, and this time she met his fire with a fire of her own, then she tore away and ran into the house.

Mike stood in the murk making a cigarette. His hands shook, the paper tore and he cast the cigarette aside with a soft oath.

When Antonia came out with the shawl lying loosely around her shoulders she said: "Do you have a ring?"

"A ring? No, but I can—"

"Here." She held out her hand, palm up. A heavy gold band lay there. "It was my mother's."

He took it saying: "Is this what you want, Toni? Because, if you'd rather I—"

"That's exactly what I want, Mike. That, and you."

They started down off the porch and starlight dappled them with soft silver; around them darkness lay warmly soft and hushed.

Center Point Publishing

600 Brooks Road ● PO Box 1
Thorndike ME 04986-0001 USA

(207) 568-3717

**US & Canada:
1 800 929-9108**